EVERYTHING
BREAKS

EVERYTHING BREAKS

VICKI GROVE

G. P. PUTNAM'S SONS
AN IMPRINT OF PENGUIN GROUP (USA) INC.

G. P. PUTNAM'S SONS
An imprint of Penguin Young Readers Group.
Published by The Penguin Group.
Penguin Group (USA) Inc., 375 Hudson Street, New York, NY 10014, USA

USA | Canada | UK | Ireland | Australia | New Zealand | India | South Africa | China
Penguin Books Ltd, Registered Offices: 80 Strand, London WC2R 0RL, England
For more information about the Penguin Group, visit penguin.com

Library of Congress Cataloging-in-Publication Data
Grove, Vicki. Everything breaks / Vicki Grove. pages cm
Summary: After his three best friends die in a car crash when he should have
been driving, seventeen-year-old Tucker meets Charon, the Ferryman of Hades,
and must decide whether to succumb to his grief or go on living.
[1. Grief—Fiction. 2. Best friends—Fiction. 3. Friendship—Fiction. 4. Charon
(Greek mythology)—Fiction. 5. Quapaw Indians—Fiction. 6. Indians of North America—
Oklahoma—Fiction. 7. Supernatural—Fiction.] I. Title.
PZ7.G9275Eve 2013 [Fic]—dc23 2013014190

Published simultaneously in Canada. Printed in the United States of America.
ISBN 978-0-399-25088-0
1 3 5 7 9 10 8 6 4 2

Text set in Maxime Std.

In loving memory of my dad,
Jim Baum (1920–2010).
He could fix anything, and he never let us leave home
without good tread on our tires and all the right tools in the trunk.

EVERYTHING BREAKS

1

IT WASN'T EVEN supposed to happen. The bonfire, that is. It was supposed to be rained out. I mean it *could* have been. There was a tropical storm off the coast of Texas that the TV weathercasters kept saying was supposed to come north and hit Oklahoma.

But late Saturday afternoon, the storm veered east instead. Bud and I were watching a game on TV when the all-clear bulletin crawled across the bottom of the screen. I was waiting for Trey to pick me up for the bonfire or wherever else we'd decide to go if it was called off, and Bud was just sitting in his La-Z-Boy recliner, like always.

My stepmother, Janet, was at her waitressing job, and I was hanging with Bud because he'd been kind of low lately and Janet had asked me to give him some company while she was gone. Otherwise I would probably have been texting about if anyone knew if the bonfire was still happening. Then after that maybe I'd have been out in the hoop house, cutting back the ankle-breaking recent explosion of pumpkin vines.

Bud was Janet's father. He came with the package when my dad married Janet back when I was eight. When my dad left us three years later, the package shrank to just Bud, Janet, and me. I quit thinking about the man some time ago. My dad, I mean. I don't remember too much about my mother either. She died when I was little, but Janet has a photo of her hanging on the living room wall, where you can see it.

In that picture, she's definitely Quapaw. My father, wherever he might be, is half Quapaw as well. To describe myself, I'd say I'm pretty much Quapaw, straight black hair, black eyes. I run track, so I've got a runner's build. Not a lot of meat on my bones. I like to feel in control like you do on a five-mile run when everything's in rhythm and your thoughts aren't chewing on themselves like something trapped and desperate.

Several girls I've dated have complained that they never know what I'm thinking. Trey threw back his head and howled when I mentioned that to him. "Dude! Don't you even know that about yourself?" Then he got serious and said quietly, "Tucker, you keep yourself tight, but so would I if what happened to you had happened to me."

The thing is, Trey always knew what I was thinking *without* my telling him. When my mother died and Trey and I were six, he helped me tie her tribal bracelet into my hair, where eleven years later that colored band of tiny shell beads remains tangled into the strand in back I keep longer for that purpose. Over the years he had to retie it for me a few times, and once he restrung the beads and feather when the leather had frayed.

2

Then when we were eleven and my dad left, Trey waited a few months until it was for sure he wasn't coming back, then organized a ceremony to separate me from him. He called it an exorcism, after this movie we'd both seen, and he said stuff about him he'd mostly learned in Sunday school and from Star Wars videos. Stuff like "we banish thee to hyperspace where Moses shall smite thee for thy transgressions against this Jedi, thy son Tucker." Since I couldn't bring myself to think anything about my dad, it was a great comfort to have Trey doing it for me. Trey had made us lightsabers for that ceremony that he carved from maple branches like he later did his favorite drumsticks, and we crossed them, then battled with them until they were shredded back to mere sticks and we had a few satisfying scratches. My stomach had been aching in a weird way until that ceremony. It settled some secret feelings I'd been carrying and made me feel calmer.

"This'll be the last bonfire of our junior year," I mentioned to Bud when we saw that all-clear weather bulletin on TV. "Would've been too bad if it'd got rained out. Everybody's psyched."

Bud whistled a bit of something through his teeth, then said, "Woulda, coulda, shoulda." He curved his hairy hands and tapped his long nails on the chair arms a few times, which was another thing that worried Janet, not because it meant Bud was depressed but because it was shredding the upholstery. "Woulda, coulda, shoulda," he repeated. "Makes no difference once the fiddler stops the music and turns out the lights."

It wasn't easy piecing Bud's old guy–isms together. Once the fiddler . . . what?

Trey honked for me. I jumped up and maneuvered around sleeping Ringo, then grabbed my jacket from the closet. "Later, Bud. I'm off to the bonfire."

Bud raised a hand in farewell, and I was out the front door and down the porch stairs in three or four strides. But once I'd loped across the street and had the passenger-side door of the Mustang open, Trey called across, "Hey, come around and drive, will you?"

I swallowed my shock and bent to get a better look at his face, trying to see if he was just messing with me. He had his wallet spread against the steering wheel and was excavating deep for something. His expression was at first hidden behind the curtain of his long red hair, then I guess he saw my shadow falling over him. "Hey, man," he turned to greet me, nodding in recognition as though I had just that second walked up.

Then he went back to his intense scavenge through his grungy wallet.

Trey, his crazy tangle of hair in a constant state of flux and his nearly transparent skin stretched across the wide bones of his face, his long drummer's fingers always moving, always fluid. Trey, so innocently and genuinely shocked when something went missing, not ever once realizing that it happened to him all the time, at least daily, almost hourly.

Actually, Trey was sort of a flake, though it was the last thing people would have thought. He was one of the most take-charge guys in school, in complete control when a bully needed to be put down or a drum needed to be played or, well, when the Mustang had showed up in pieces at the junkyard. But he routinely left behind his sunglasses, his money, his jacket, his little sister who waited for him patiently wherever he was supposed to pick her up. He never remembered to study, never memorized his locker combination, lost five or six phones before he finally gave up on his ability to have a phone and just started borrowing my phone or Zero's when he needed one. He often had no concept of what day or month it was, or, on Saturdays, whether it was noon or midnight. He lived in the present, minute by minute, and I admired that. But I occasionally worried that his innocent carelessness might get him into real trouble someday.

"You're not serious about the driving, right?" I quietly asked him.

He'd restored that vintage red convertible himself and nobody touched it, ever.

"Yeah, man, take the wheel so I can do this thing," he grumbled in a friendly way, propelling himself and his wallet over the gearshift panel and into the passenger seat without looking up. "It's *gotta* be in here someplace." His tone, as usual in this sort of situation, was of total disbelief, as if his horribly bulging wallet was perfectly organized and functional.

I ran around and slid into the driver's seat. Late-afternoon shadows were painting the Mustang's white leather seats the color Janet calls lavender blue. It's the sort of mellow shade that lulls you into thinking nothing bad can happen in life, which now seems like a wicked joke, considering what *did* happen only a few hours later.

I remember that I felt truly fine myself, driving that truly fine machine. I was pure muscle and bone, nothing more. I felt simple and happy as an animal, maybe a wolf or coyote, moving swiftly across the warm earth under the cool October sky.

As we cruised through the neighborhood, Trey kept throwing bits of wallet junk out the window and into the gulley that dribbles through our subdivision. A few old ticket stubs, some pictures of girls, a damp-looking book of matches.

Finally, he maneuvered out an accordioned twenty and kissed it, then waggled it in my face and yelled, "Tucker, my man, I found it! It's party time!"

I gave him a grin as I eased the car toward the curb, figuring he'd want the wheel back. But he motioned for me to keep going, extravagant in his generosity now that he'd found that twenty. If I saw this right, it had been stuck to the back of an Ozzie Smith baseball card by a leftover bit of some smashed candy bar he'd been saving in his wallet. I think it was a Snickers, his favorite. Not that it matters. Nothing like that matters now.

He switched on his music. It was System of a Down, and he began finger-drumming the complicated beat. Trey played with various bands in the summer and sometimes on weekends. He was the real thing and actually got paid for drumming. The rest of us felt lucky to flip burgers in fast-food places or, in my case, to do landscaping in the summer for Greenfield's, selling

Christmas trees there during the holidays, sorting seeds and planting seedlings most weekends in the spring.

"Get Zero first, then Steve!" Trey called above the thump of his fine retro speaker system. "Then take us to that SpeedMart out on West Fork. I brought my brother's ID, but I probably won't need it since my cousin Leo will be working tonight. Everybody else asked off for the bonfire."

I picked up speed on the stretch of asphalt leading to Zero's trailer park at the edge of town. The wind sheered along my left elbow where it finned outside the open window. Night was coming on and everything felt so right, so good and so free. I even thought about howling, like Trey was doing.

But Trey was always the howler of the two of us, so I just grinned instead.

The Vagabond Park is a dusty field of pale trailers set up on concrete blocks in small patches of brown grass, but there's an exciting neon sign at the entrance—a huge, flashing pink and green palm tree. Zero said he thought that sign had dazzled his mother, that and the name of the place. He expected her to move them once she noticed the blandness of her surroundings, but when she and Zero had been in Clevesdale for a few months, she instead behaved like the true artist she is and transformed their trailer to match the sign.

We helped, Trey and I. It was the summer between eighth and ninth grade and Steve hadn't moved here yet. Zero's mother got a bunch of blue paint, I remember it was called Electric

Turquoise, and once we had the trailer covered in three coats of that, she detailed it out with orange paint in a fringe around the windows and door, then welded big metal starfish and sea horses here and there. She painted a mermaid on the propane tank at the edge of the yard. Some people at the Vagabond put lattice around their ugly gas tanks in a weak attempt to hide them, but Zero's mother drew attention to hers, turning it into a striking piece of sculpture. That's the way she does things. You get it or you don't.

We nailed together a big wooden porch to cover the front portion of brown grass. Zero painted it purple. On that front porch is always a steel drum that Zero's mother actually knows how to play and, after some serious nagging by him, taught Trey to play as well. Also six or seven of Zero's skateboards, and several iron vats his mother uses to cook her dye for the batik dresses and wall hangings she sells online.

There are two mimosa trees in Zero's backyard and one in the front, all planted by his mother three years ago. The one in front grows through a jagged hole we hacked in the porch floor. His mother has tiny colored lights woven through all their branches because she says that reminds her of her childhood home in Haiti.

It was dusky enough that the lights were twinkling in the front porch mimosa by the time we got to Zero's that afternoon to pick him up for the bonfire. He was sitting cross-legged on the porch floor, streamlining one of his skateboards with his serious-looking pocketknife. He carefully wiped that tool and pocketed it, then just as carefully replaced that board. Only then did he turn to us and punch the darkening sky with both fists.

"Dudes! The bonfire is *on!*" he shouted, running to the Stang and diving into the backseat through the window. Zero never took the time to enter anything by a door.

Zero and his dreadlocks, his ever-present cutoffs exposing white scars that ran like hieroglyphs up and down his muscular brown legs, telling the proud stories of his many excruciating skateboard wipeouts. Something came ahead of him, always. Or maybe I mean something floated around him. He stirred the air. All that smartness, all those scars, those moving dreads. Zero popped out at you and made you jump back a step.

"Hey, Tucker's driving!" Zero's head appeared in a sort of energy burst between our front seats. "Whassup with that, huh?" He looked from me to Trey then back to me.

"Yeah," I agreed as I shifted down, cornered under the flashing palm tree and bumped out onto the road to Steve's. "I dunno why Trey's letting me," I added.

I indeed was driving, and I couldn't stop grinning about it.

"This being our last bonfire of the year," Trey explained in a drifty way, focused more on the music coming from the speakers than on his answer. "This being our last one of those, young Tucker, whose legendary innocence is, well, you know, pretty much legendary, will be our chauffeur tonight, which we've never had before because there's always more. More bonfires. More lake parties and what have you. Now, there won't be more, not junior year, and everybody knows junior year is best. Junior year. Party year."

I did a quick translation. They'd be drinking more than usual tonight.

Zero pushed back to sprawl in his seat. I glanced in the rearview mirror and saw that his eyes were sparking as he stared out the window. His arms were stretched wide along the top of the seat and he was jittering his fingers. His quick-fire mind was already on to the next thing. Me being the driver had been left behind in the dust.

"I'm flying down Hawk's Slope soon!" he called up to us above the wind that was now rushing through our open windows. Steve's ranch was several miles out and I was giving it the gas. "I wanta get to the top tonight so I can eyeball any major crevasses and figure my angle of descent, then I'll graph it out and probably fly it next week, before we get our first freeze and the gravel makes a big shift."

I'd better explain right here that Zero was probably a science genius, far beyond Clevesdale High's ability to school him. In fact, Zero was the reason Mr. Philbrick, the Boeing engineer he met at space camp back in junior high, left money in his will for the skateboard park at the north edge of our town. Zero had actually convinced Mr. Philbrick that skateboarding was a kind of three-dimensional physics, not that Zero ever practiced his constant experiments at that particular place, the Philbrick Skate Park.

No, Zero preferred more challenging venues for his carefully graphed-out skateboard flights, like the steps of the post office. Or the silver mountains of gravel that rise around the abandoned zinc mines a few miles outside of town, which is where we'd be headed once we'd picked up Steve and gone back to town to get beer at SpeedMart.

Zero had flown his skateboard down all the gravel mountains but one, the one he'd just mentioned to us in a shouted but casual way. Hawk's Slope. In a certain sense, he knew what he was doing. But again, how *could* he know what he was doing when what he was doing was something so outrageous?

Hawk's Slope is a treacherous gravel mountain, a monster built of tons of zinc mine leavings that looms a good two hundred feet high. Even four-wheeler fanatics respect the Hawk and lay their trails only along the bottom third of it. It's not easy to climb even in the daytime, the gravel tumbles and heaves so much. You slide back down as much as you make progress. People break legs and arms trying to get to the top. That hadn't happened to any of the four of us, so we figured it only happened to fools. But even the local dirt bikers had pretty much had their fill of pain and now left the Hawk alone.

Because the zinc mine fields were near the lake, we went there to do our pre-bonfire drinking, but definitely not to do night climbing up the gravel mountains. Everything about this latest Zero plan was too sudden, too extreme, and too illegal.

"Aren't you gonna try and talk me out of it?" Zero had popped forward again to yell the question right at me, teasing me for worrying like they all three did upon occasion.

11

"We're late already for the bonfire without climbing, that's all," I murmured.

Trey reached with an elbow to pry Zero back a few inches, yelling in his good-natured way, "Hey, save what you're saying for the party, man! Nobody can hear you with Tucker racing the devil like this!"

Racing the devil. It was a strange thing to say, wasn't it? Something from a movie, probably. Trey liked movies, even really old ones.

Zero disappeared from my peripheral vision, and the next time I glanced into the mirror, he was twiddling his fingers with his eyes slightly glazed again, planning.

You're driving alongside Steve's stepfather's land for miles before you see the huge gates of the ranch. Those iron gates are hardly ever closed, but if you dare drive through them, there are surveillance cameras watching you all the time, hidden in the trees along the half-mile lane leading to Jasper Nordike's sprawling mansion of a ranch house.

I'm not saying I know what qualifies as a mansion. But Janet's been in that house a few times to cater parties and that's what she calls it.

"I felt like I was at the White House, it was so beautiful," she told me the first time she came back from being over there. "That music room where Cynthia keeps her harp and grand piano? Oh, my. And those collections she has, all that bone china in that huge walnut buffet, and I guess my favorite was that antique cabinet displaying those little glass thatched houses from her trips to England."

Which is where her husband met the tour guide who's now his trophy wife, I could hardly keep from saying. To occupy my mouth, I took another of the little leftover crepe things she'd brought back from that fancy party Steve's mother had thrown.

"There's six bedrooms in that house," Janet went on. "Each with its own big-screen television set and its own bathroom, all with jetted tubs. It's been featured in six decorator magazines." She sighed like a dazzled little girl. "They even have a bowling alley in the basement. But you know all about it, Tuck, being good friends with Steve."

I'd never been in the ranch house. Steve doesn't ever go in it unless he's forced to.

Three years ago, his mother had been playing harp with a small orchestra at a cattlemen's convention in Memphis when she met Jasper Nordike, the third-largest rancher in Oklahoma. They married and Steve had to move here from Memphis right in the middle of ninth grade. You only had to hear Steve take out his battered clarinet and play some Memphis blues to understand completely how he felt about that sudden move.

Since Steve grew up on horseback, Jasper Nordike was happy to let him help with the ranch, working cattle in the summers and a lot of school-year afternoons. They use several full-time hands, so there's a bunkhouse, and Steve begged and pleaded until finally his mother gave up and let him move his stuff out there.

He ate breakfast in the bunkhouse, did his share of cooking, and only visited the ranch house for supper sometimes, not very often. In the bunkhouse he slept in a top bunk, one of six narrow beds, three sets of bunks, all in the same room with a small television, a kitchenette, and hooks for gear and clothes lining the log walls. There's one shower stall for all six ranch hands. Being clean isn't a huge priority.

Steve had movie star cowboy looks to begin with, and they only got worse until by this year most of the girls in our class were either sick with longing for him or furious with him for dating them then dropping them with no explanation. His white-blond hair was always sweat spiked in random directions, set off by his all-year tan. He wore his jeans for so many days that they became fitted. His boots, relics from Memphis, had the broken-in look boots only get when you've done years of crazy things in them.

"Steved" is what we enviously called the reaction he caused when he slouched down the halls of Clevesdale High. Those poor girls he passed had been "Steved."

He didn't realize how handsome he was, or care. The word around school was that Steve was too vain and too choosy to date a girl more than once or twice. But he was the farthest thing from vain, and the only choice that truly mattered to him had been taken away when his mother remarried and moved him to Clevesdale, Oklahoma. He dreamed so constantly of moving back to Memphis that it was clear to Zero, Trey, and me that he didn't have the heart or head space left over to care about much beyond that.

I slowed the Mustang to a crawl as we turned off the paved entrance lane to the ranch house and onto the rutted dirt road leading to the stables and the bunkhouse.

There was Steve, leaning against a fencepost with his boots crossed at the ankle, playing his clarinet. He raised one arm in our direction to say he saw us, then took off his hat and sailed it onto the bunkhouse porch. I thought he'd dodge inside the bunkhouse himself to stow his clarinet, but he tucked it into its ratty case and brought it with him.

"Last bonfire of the year," he explained as he hoisted that case onto the backseat and climbed in behind it. "Thought I'd play us some music in honor of that, out at the zinc mines. When I first got good enough to play blues, I used to play 'St. Louie Woman' from the roof of the Peabody Hotel sometimes, just as the sun set over the Mississippi."

Zero snorted. "You are one seriously sentimental dude."

Trey and I were smiling at that as I carefully turned the car and took us back over the dirt trail of a road to its junction with Jasper Nordike's smooth entrance drive.

I let the car idle there for a minute because the dozens of automatic lights surrounding the ranch house had just come on. From this distance the place looked like a castle from a kids' book, or maybe a cathedral like in Europe. It drew all our eyes.

"Dude, I would live *there*," Zero told Steve. "I'd bowl every single night."

At first Steve said nothing. Then, "It's a real treasure house, all right," he allowed. "But everything cost *so* much. My mother tells anyone who'll listen that most of it's one of a kind and can't be replaced. Who can get comfortable in a place like that, where you can't quit looking around and thinking how *easy* everything breaks?"

II

AT THE SPEEDMART, Zero and I waited in the car while Trey and Steve started in to get the beer. "Guard my instrument!" Steve called back to Zero before the big double doors whooshed shut behind them.

Zero and I shook our heads and had a quick laugh at Steve thinking anyone would have an interest in his grungy old instrument case. Then Zero pushed himself forward.

"Admit that you're worrying about my climb tonight, Tuck," he demanded, giving my shoulder a little shake. "Come on, just admit it."

What difference did it make? I shrugged. "It'll be totally dark by the time we're out there, too dangerous for the Hawk. And we *are* already late for the bonfire."

"I knew it!" He gave a sort of triumphant cackle as he slid back to his own place. "Tucker, you innocent wonder, our lives are random, don't you get that? A coin is flipped each time you walk outside—heads you get to eat your favorite pizza, tails you get hit by a bus on the way to the pizza place. So you might as well get loose, dude. Maybe drink a few beers tonight, you know? Quit worrying so much! Have *fun!*"

I leaned forward and pushed my forehead against the hard black plastic of the steering wheel, letting Trey's music thump its way directly into my brain. Why was Zero's banter getting to me? It was just Zero being Zero. Besides, maybe he was right.

I'd tried drinking a couple of beers on two different occasions the fall of sophomore year. Beer tasted to me like something gone off, and I couldn't stand the feeling it gave me of not being able to handle myself. So I gave up trying to get into it, and my function since was to sit watch on the deep chrome fender of the Mustang while the other three drank, ready to give them a whistled signal if the police or one of Steve's angry ex-girlfriends materialized while they were whooping it up in the zinc mine fields. That was how I had gained the "innocent wonder" nickname, though, a nickname that was starting, I suddenly realized, to get really and truly old.

Steve and Trey came out carrying two squared-off sacks. Steve threw his toward Zero and Zero reached out his window and snatched it from the air.

"That hopeless Leo carded me after all. Can you believe it? His own cousin!" Trey shook his head at the outrage as he dropped his package through the passenger-side window and went to join Steve, who was already at work pushing back and stowing the convertible's white vinyl top.

When they finished, Trey came toward the driver's side, pulling his wild new-penny hair back into a rubber band he'd found on the sidewalk. I opened my door to let him have the wheel, but he just shook his head and threw the pack of cigs he'd just bought next to his green lighter on the floor between the door and seat where he kept that stuff. Then he ran around the car, finger-drumming a happy little riff on the hood as he went.

He dropped back into the passenger seat. "Drive on, young Tucker, you innocent wonder. You can be our designated driver!" He slammed his door and ripped into the box on the floor between his feet. "The rest of us can get a head start on these babies on the way out there!" he called over his shoulder.

I stared at the metallic blue of the cardboard box Trey was tearing apart. *The rest of us,* Trey had just said. Everyone knew junior year was the best, and this was our last bonfire of the year. I could swallow down some beer, why not?

"Tuck? You okay, dude?"

I flinched and looked up to meet Trey's innocent, friendly eyes.

"Yeah, yeah, sure. Just save a couple of those for me, for when we get there."

Trey punched me, happy at the news. I turned the key, and by the time we pulled from the SpeedMart parking lot, they were all guzzling their first beers.

True night comes on fast in October once the sun sinks, so the moon was up and shining like a quarter by the time we bumped onto the rock road to the zinc mine fields. Ahead of us loomed our homegrown mountains of excavated gravel, with Hawk's

Slope shining high and serene above the rest. I let the Mustang roll along in neutral as Trey always did here, and before long we could feel the shock of the slippery clay that meant we were now right on top of the hollowed-out and then abandoned underground mines.

I gently toed the brake, and before the car had glided to a complete stop, Zero and Steve scrambled out and began jumping up and down to feel the hollow ground shuddering in response. Steve grabbed a rock and dropped it down one of the air-shaft holes, and we all heard the eerie flute-like sound of its long descent to what sounded like it might be the center of the earth.

"Hey, guys, we got the place to ourselves!" Zero shouted.

We'd been running late. Everyone else who'd done their pre-bonfire drinking out here must have already moved on to the lake, where the fire was set.

"Y'all look over at the sky, right above the bluff!" Steve yelled. "It's that crazy light thing, that Oreo boardless thing!"

We all turned toward where Seneca Bluff rose like a high backbone between the zinc mine fields and Chisum Lake. It was too dark to actually see the bluff, but we could tell where it was. It blotted out a long section of stars like some gigantic prehistoric monster.

"Aurora borealis," Zero casually corrected Steve. "But that light in the clouds is just a reflection of the bonfire. You can see it tonight because the clouds are low and the rest of the sky has gotten so black."

There was an old access road that connected the zinc mine

fields to the lake. It looked like a crazy belt around Seneca Bluff, zigzagging nearly vertically up this side of that sleeping monster then zigzagging just as crazily down the lake side. The road was treacherous and had been officially closed for years, though the chain blocking its entrance had at some point been cut in half, probably by bonfire parties. Most people took the long road around the bluff to reach the bonfires, but there were a few who considered the nerly vertical little forbidden access road to be a pre-bonfire thrill ride, especially if they were running late, or were showing off, or both.

Trey ordinarily took the long road, worried mostly about scraping the Mustang's paint against the bluff's limestone surface. It could happen, the access road was that narrow in places. He'd taken the access road a couple of times when we felt the need to hurry, though. Tonight, we were already late and Zero was running toward the Hawk, beers cradled in his shirt, yelling crazy things and laughing. No question, he was climbing, which meant we were all climbing.

We'd take the shortcut over the bluff when we'd drunk our beer and satisfied Zero. It was a given if we wanted to get there before the party began to wind down.

Steve lifted his clarinet case and headed off into the darkness with it. Trey and I stayed in the car, shaking our heads at Zero's nutty enthusiasm. Trey glowed in the darkness, ghostly pale as the moon, still drumming his fingers to a beat in his head.

I watched my hand take a beer from the package on the floor between his feet. I drank it in one grimacing swallow, then took a second can with me and choked most of it down as I got out of the car. I heard Trey's door slam too as I jogged to join Zero.

"Hey, hey!" Zero noticed the can dangling from my fingers when I came close, and nodded appreciatively. "Here." He stuck one of his own beers into my free hand, then grabbed my elbow and began dragging me behind him. "Now, c'mon, Tucker, let's climb this mountain before it gets to looking even higher!"

I broke free of his grip and paused to turn myself in a slow circle on my heel, looking up at the sky as I drained that second can. White stars began entering the night like popcorn. White stars entering like popcorn. That image seemed so beautiful, perfect, and even, yes, wise. Who knew you became a poet when you drank?

And then I was climbing, fast, faster than I'd ever dared climb Hawk's Slope. I could see Zero speeding along above me, with his moving dreads a cloud of darker darkness against the night sky. I looked down through my legs and saw Trey climbing a few yards below me, dodging the trickle of small rocks I was dislodging. My boots were throwing sparks as they shifted the gravel, and I wondered if I had magical powers. One thing I was sure of, you became a better climber when your brain was deactivated so you didn't worry about falling or causing an avalanche.

I told myself to remember that, when I was sober again.

"Whoo, woo—eee!" Zero sang above me. "I wanta fly right into this black, black night. I wanta ride this sky like an eagle!"

I twisted around, then flipped over, digging my heels

into the gravel so I could lie back against the steep slope like Zero was doing, like we'd all learned to do when we wanted a quick rest from slogging our way up the loose gravel. The view was incredible at night. Everything on the ground looked insignificant and you could see the lights of several towns that were miles away.

A few yards beneath me, Trey had turned to rest as well. I could glimpse his bright hair through my feet. "Look at Steve!" he called up to Zero and me. "Can you see him, down there to the left of the car?"

Steve was standing in one of the few splotches of moonlight not shadowed by the mountains. His battered instrument case was a tiny rectangle at his feet and he had his clarinet in his hands. And then he began to play.

And as the sly, lovelorn notes of "St. Louie Woman" come gliding up that silver mountain with the stars ticking through the universe and the wind turning cold but the rocks beneath our backs holding their heat, I felt something true and elemental and knew the others were feeling it as well and that none of us would ever forget how we felt at that exact moment. A car-obsessed, heedless drummer and a science-loving daredevil, a heartbroken cowboy and a silent Indian. The four of us, authentic as our individual selves and authentic together. I wanted to feel exactly like this forever.

We howled and applauded when Steve finished, which is when I noticed that that third beer was still, unbelievably, in my hand. How I'd climbed with it I didn't know, but I popped it and drank it down, then twisted back around to keep climbing.

But I suddenly felt so dizzy that a red flash of fear hit my heart. I twisted to face outward again, but then I felt like I was about to slide right off the world.

"I think I'll go on down now," I managed to tell Trey when he came up even.

I could tell my forced nonchalance didn't fool him, but he asked no questions, merely nodded. "I better follow Zero to hurry him along," he said. "But hey, man, take it real slow and easy going down, okay?"

The moon was a sort of nightmare sun that cast jagged, disorienting shadows everywhere I looked. I half crawled, half slid back down, and when I finally landed, I picked a spot of glare that I thought might be the chrome fender of the Mustang. I tried to run straight to it and, a bit to my surprise, I eventually reached the car.

I flopped into the backseat and covered my eyes with my arms.

"No way can I drive," I groaned pitifully to myself, forgetting that I wasn't alone.

A few seconds later I heard Steve yell toward the mountain, "Hey, Tuck's down and he ain't looking so good! Y'all had better come on back so's we can get on goin' to where we're supposed to be goin'!"

I must have passed out or something then, because the next thing I heard or felt was the car bumping along a rock road. We were climbing at a tilt that was crazy steep, which meant we must have been nearing the apex of our cruise up and over Seneca Bluff.

I cracked open one eye and saw that Steve was in the back with me, politely squeezing himself against the door since I was taking up most of the seat.

I forced myself to sit up and give him some room, but that turned out not to be a good idea. I jerked forward to yell into Trey's ear, "Stop! Stop and . . . let me out! I gotta puke!" It came on really fast, like I guess it usually does.

Trey swerved across the road to get to the narrow left shoulder in about one second, screaming, "Don't puke in my car! Don't you dare puke in my car, Graysten!"

Then even as the Mustang still rocked in the loose gravel, I propelled myself out of the roofless car and into the ditch, vomiting at the same split second my knees hit the ground.

"Go on!" I yelled when I could get a breath. "I'll catch you later, down at the party!"

I managed a good-natured wave and they drove on with a screech of fine whitewall tires. I was grateful to have the privacy to do my necessary heaving. I figured that later I could run the last mile or two of the road, where it went straight along the very top of the bluff, then veered around a final sharp switchback curve and started downward, toward the beach. There are times when being a runner comes in real handy, and this would be one of them.

But the heaving turned out to be the least of it. I kept trying to force the moonlit mud and brown grass to hold still and form some sort of sense, but everything just kept spinning around. *I am completely wasted,* I admitted to myself.

I sat down hard in the prickly grass and pulled up my knees so I could prop my elbows on them. I wove my fingers through my hair, trying to keep my skull from blowing off as I concentrated on figuring out exactly where I was. From the level feel of the ground, I figured Trey had deposited me on the stretch of narrow asphalt that ran for a little way along the high spine of the bluff road. I would have this half-mile or so of even and easy running before a line of five thick, white highway posts would warn me that the road was immediately taking a ninety-degree turn and then a plunge. I would have to give up my nice flat jog at that point and run a stomach-wrenching series of downward zig-zags that would finally deposit me on the beach.

Two hundred feet below where I huddled right now, a large percentage of the junior and senior class was partying. The bonfire cast tall, flickering shadows on the thick oak trees that lined the side of the road where I'd been puking. The other side of the road was spangled with scraggly little bushes that disguised the edge of the bluff, the steep drop down to the beach. If I could drag myself the fifteen feet or so from where I sat over to that hazardous edge, I knew I could look straight down and see the reassuring sight of everyone dancing far below, their shadows gigantic on the rocky sand. The dark lake would be tonguing at the shore mere feet from them in a friendly, mutt-like way.

I thought it was a bit strange that I was hearing no music, but I couldn't hold on to that thought. What I *did* hear was plenty of raised voices, lots of shouting, lots of raucous humans being raucous humans on the last October Saturday night of the year.

I kept trying to stand and stay standing, and finally, I made it. I started my lurching run through the darkness with flickering bonfire shadows animating the trees on my left and party noise coming at me from far below, on my right.

Party noise that surely didn't, if I'd been sober enough to notice, sound anything at all like carefree and music-filled party noise. Now, I realize I was hearing screams.

I settled into a sort of half jog, ignoring the clanging in my ears and the way the dark road undulated and heaved like some long black rug Janet had taken in her strong waitress hands and was snapping viciously free of grime. The stars bore down on me like leaks in the black sky.

Then, straight ahead and ghostly, were the five white highway markers that warned of that sudden sharp turn. The moon clearly picked out each one of them, but… something just wasn't *right*.

I pushed closer, then stopped, panting, my hands on my knees and my eyes squinted in disbelief. The white posts had always been as straight and upright as five little soldiers standing at attention, but now they were splayed crazily at strange, uneven angles. They were . . . broken or something. A couple of them might even have gone missing.

Then suddenly this huge, dark *thing* sailed across the road a few yards in front of me, blocking out the stars for maybe four seconds as it flew from high up in the trees on the left side of the road to land in a patch of darkness between two of those messed-up posts!

Was it some gigantic bird? A flock of big birds? The quick but loose way the thing had moved through the air was somehow unnatural, like a shadow or a dark mist.

I fumbled for the small LED flashlight I keep dangling from my belt loop. I focused its intense beam on the place between the two messed-up posts where I'd seen the thing land. At first there was nothing but bare, weedy grass with twinkling stars in the background. And then, as I watched in total disbelief, this . . . this *dog* began to appear. I mean, it just slowly, well, *materialized* there in the grass between those two posts!

The dog was large and sleek, a black dog about the size of Ringo, our old golden Lab. No, it was actually bigger than Ringo. Much bigger.

It looked straight at me with its tongue out in that eager way dogs look at you when they're waiting for you to feed them or walk them or something. It seemed so friendly that I would have tried hard to chalk up all its strange actions to my being wasted. But there was one thing about it that would have been as hard for my aching brain to make up as it was for it to forget. The dog had too many heads. Two too many. Three in all.

I dropped to my knees, staring in openmouthed disbelief, confused and afraid. The dog took that as a gesture of friendship, grinned a doggy grin—three doggy grins—and began moving toward me in a sort of slow-motion lope.

It got so close I could see the details of its large, luminous eyes, and I heard myself give a little whimper. Something was swimming inside each of the six of them! I groped with numb fingers for my forgotten flashlight and dared to aim it directly at the right eye in the dog's closest head. It had no iris. Instead, a tiny spiral was slowly whirling around the eye's dark pupil.

This had to be a hallucination or *some*thing. I closed my own eyes tight as I could and hammered my forehead with my knuckles until I could feel those thuds through the numbness in my brain.

When I dared to open them again, the dog was gone without a trace.

But the posts hadn't come back into the straight, even line they had to be in.

The moon came out from behind a cloud so suddenly that I almost screamed. It gave a blast of light to the white posts and I saw several loose and tangled lengths of the thick, corded steel wire that usually held the posts upright and taut, making them into a safety barrier it would be hard to break through.

Those pieces of useless, broken wire were now bobbing gently in the night air like the windblown stems of gigantic, flowerless plants.

I got up, stumbled to the nearest white post, held on to it and looked down.

Everything in me went electric and I dropped to a sit, pushed off and slip-slid down that nearly vertical limestone bluff. I got hung up two or three times on little trees that grew straight out from the stone. Maybe I felt my flesh ripping along the way, tearing like the denim of my jeans was tearing. Maybe I felt it, or maybe I didn't. I can't remember. All I remember is that my eyes stung with the rising smoke of burning gasoline when I was partway down but I couldn't close them for even a second because I had to watch and watch and watch like in a nightmare you have to watch and watch and watch.

Directly below that switchback curve and down the beach a little way from the bonfire, the burning Mustang was planted up to its windshield in the gravelly sand.

THE FIRE WAS MORE ALIVE than anything I'd ever seen. It was a wildly beautiful creature made of flame and with the mindless energy of a demon, and it had pounced directly on Trey's car and was sinking long claws and razor fangs deep into the steel and glass and the smoking tires.

When my feet hit the sand, I started running blindly toward the thing, screaming Trey's name, yelling at him to throw it into reverse and give it the gas and get out of there. My legs were numb and uncoordinated and the sand got hotter the nearer I came until I could feel the soles of my feet blistering right through my boots. But I somehow thought that I could pry open the burning doors and pull them free so they could run clear of the fire, maybe bruised and bumped around a bit, but still . . . themselves. Yes, I pictured myself freeing my friends, then all four of us would run to safety, propping each other up and laughing in a horrified, slaphappy way about the too-close call.

For a while, the police didn't notice me any more than I noticed them, I guess because they were busy keeping most of

Clevesdale's junior and senior class behind sawhorse barricades along the beach. I managed to get really close to the Mustang, so close it hurt to breathe. I put my arm over my nose and mouth and moved even closer, then through the wall of smoke I actually glimpsed Trey, his hands on the wheel. Yes, his hands on the wheel! He might yet give the engine some gas and get out of this. Trey was famous for successful last-ditch efforts. Eking out a D-minus on a final exam he couldn't afford to fail. Charming some girl's parents into believing he'd brought their daughter home two hours late because of a highway detour. Getting the very last tickets for a concert everybody thought was sold out. Trey's luck was legendary.

"Hurry, man!" I screamed to him, though I couldn't hear my own words. The fire itself was deafening, and there was a sort of high screeching sound coming from the car. "Trey, gun it!" I yelled. "Get out of there, man! Give it all you've got, do it *now!*"

The car began giving off puffs of fire from somewhere deep inside itself, protesting its death by spewing clots of solid flame. Blast furnace heat arose from all directions. I smelled my eyebrows and eyelashes scorching.

And then, just before the fire exploded upward to completely engulf the car, the black smoke around the windows became white and nearly transparent and I had a much clearer view of Trey.

But I couldn't comprehend what I was seeing.

If I'd stayed a few seconds longer, I probably would have gone up in flames myself, but my shirt was grabbed from behind and

I was yanked several yards backward by what turned out to be a policeman. "What do you think you're doing?" he screamed when we were clear of the worst of the heat. "How'd you get over here on this side of the vehicle?"

He shone his flashlight in my face.

"I . . . came down the bluff," I said. I doubted if he could hear me. All the sound in the world was being sucked into what had now become the death roar of the car.

"You're making no sense, son. Nobody can come down that bluff! And look at your boots! How'd you get gasoline on them? Or wait . . . is it blood?"

But I couldn't look at my boots. Though I could no longer see anything of Trey through the new clouds of black smoke, I could see a bit of the trunk of the Mustang. I had to stand watch, to keep vigil, to keep my eyes on Trey's fine car for as long as I could see any small part of it.

Another policeman came out of the darkness behind us and took my right shoulder while the first one gripped my left elbow. "The paramedics need to check this kid out," the first one yelled across to the other one. "I'm pretty sure he's in shock, and he's bleeding from somewhere. I think his legs have been injured."

They turned me toward the beach, which seemed almost like a carnival with its many flashing lights—yellow ones on the sawhorses, red ones and blue ones atop the ambulances and police cars. I watched over my shoulder as the fire exploded upward to become a towering monster with the Mustang lost somewhere deep inside its gut.

A distant siren quickly went from loud to deafening as Clevesdale's yellow fire truck came speeding down the narrow beach road with its bells clanging and its lights whirling. It idled at the barricades just long enough for workers to scramble opening them, then it swept toward the burning car like a dragon with lidless halogen eyes.

I turned away then, from the car, from Trey. I had no choice.

A man in a yellow raincoat ran up. "We found a second body," he told the two policemen in a rushed, grim way. "Thrown from the car like the other one we found. Looks like they went down the bluff headfirst. One's probably the driver."

I couldn't feel my mouth, but I heard a strange version of my own voice saying to them, "The driver is still inside the car. His name is Trey."

Two yellow rubber tarpaulins covered something on the ground right beside the first ambulance. A breeze from the lake came up and rippled them, made it look like the long, thin bodies beneath were twitching impatiently, trying to get up and call it all a joke.

Like Zero was about to untangle his legs and rise to do a little bobbing, bent-kneed dance with his cutoffs ragged around his knees and his elbows high and aerodynamic. *I told you I could fly from this bluff like an eagle, dudes!* Like Steve was going to sit up and push his hair into sweat spikes as he scouted around for his lost clarinet case. *Hey, guys, doncha remember I told you to watch my instrument?* He'd get up off the ground, surely, any second now, give the crowd a boyish smile, swat the dust from his jeans, and begin sauntering out of here with his well-worn Memphis cowboy boots.

One of the policemen stepped in front of me, blocking my view. When I tried to see around his shoulder, he took my arm and held it, hard, stopping me.

"You're gonna have to come to the station to tell us what you know about this, son," he said, quietly and gruffly. "But first let's get those legs of yours cleaned up."

A fireman ran up to talk to the other policeman. They were speaking in low voices with their backs to me as the first policeman led me away. I wasn't supposed to hear what they were saying, but I heard all right. I could hear everything—some of the kids from my class acting hysterical, others acting like they were too cool to act hysterical, the yellow flashers on the barricades clicking on and off and on and off, the gravel squishing under the gum boots of the firemen and policemen, the lake moving, the fire moving, the stars moving in the faraway black sky.

"With a fire as hot as this one, glass and metals bond to other objects, including human remains," the fireman was saying to that policeman. "When that thing burns out, it'll be hard to tell who or what anything used to be."

I closed my eyes and saw Trey against my lids, Trey as I'd seen him when the smoke had cleared for that half second, Trey's head and arms flailing around like he was playing his drums at a gig with his band. Yes, that's what I'd thought I'd seen for that crazy half-second, Trey drumming. Now, I understood he'd been blown into jittery mock life there behind the wheel by the force of those vicious flames. His long red hair had been a glowing halo around his face, but he'd only been a puppet, a dancing and lifeless puppet. His hair had been on fire and his flesh was already becoming . . . charred.

"Here we go, son," the policeman said, and I jerked in a breath and went with him to the nearby ambulance, the one with the two yellow tarps on the ground beside it. A young guy with a fauxhawk jumped down from the back of it and headed toward us.

"I'll be back," that policeman said, then patted my shoulder and walked away.

"Hi, I'm Larry," the paramedic told me. My eyes were on those tarps as Larry cut what was left of my jeans out of the way. He gave a grim whistle and started using some sort of long-handled something to pick out the stuff that was embedded in my legs.

"Bet this smarts," Larry observed after a while. "You got enough cedar needles in you to go as a Christmas tree for Halloween next week, pal. Lots of dirt, rocks, and who knows what all. Expect a bunch of stitches when you get this all properly treated at the clinic, too. That better be tomorrow, by the way. I'll give you some painkillers for tonight, but you don't want this mess to infect."

A real wind came up, and the corner of the tarp nearest the ambulance lifted and folded itself in a neat triangle that ran diagonally about halfway across Zero's chest.

That's when I saw Zero's face. What was left of it.

"Aw, crap," Larry said, going to fix the tarp, this time battening it down at the corner with a heavy metal box from the ambulance. "Gross, huh?" he added as he walked back to me. "Just be glad it was him and not the *other* guy you saw. Nightmare stuff. You never really get all that used to it."

Larry gave me a pair of navy blue sweatpants with POLICE printed down one leg and told me to change, and when I changed, he took my shredded jeans and put them into a yellow plastic bag that also had POLICE printed on it and handed it to me.

Then the policeman returned and led me to his squad car. He put his hand on my head as I ducked into the car, just like in the movies. For a second I had a vague, hopeful notion that this *was* just a movie. I'd been sober since the moment I saw that car down on the beach, but I could barely walk or talk or remember to breathe every so often.

"Stop! I mean, we've gotta wait. We can't go yet! Where *are* they?"

He turned to me with droopy eyes and a sad and exhausted expression. "Son, they're not coming. Your friends aren't here and you're confused. Don't think about it."

I clutched the bag to my chest and tried to stop shaking. "But . . . where's the dog?" I asked under my breath, turning to stare out the window while something chilly and dark started rising in me from the feet on up.

I hoped the police would leave Janet out of it, but apparently that's not allowed when you're seventeen. She was in the waiting room at the police station, dabbing her eyes and pushing back strands of her hair that escaped the bobby pins that hold back her yellowish ponytail. She was still in her waitress uniform, and when she saw me, she jumped from her chair and started crying for real, which is exactly what I was afraid she'd do. I tried to send her a reassuring smile, but the muscles for that wouldn't work. She cried harder and moved to put her arms around me, but I sidestepped that. "I'm filthy," I murmured.

Then they led us into this small green room.

They had my old DARE officer from fifth grade ask the questions. Officer Stephens asked me how it started and I thought about that awhile, then told him with Trey honking for me and me running to the Mustang like about a thousand times before.

"Tucker and Trey have been best friends all their lives," Janet added. Her voice was trembling. She was gripping my hand between both of hers, squeezing it so hard I heard my knuckles pop. "I made both of them costumes the Halloween they were in third grade. They both wanted to be rabbits."

Trey didn't want to be just any rabbit, though, he wanted to be the Evil Trickster Rabbit. At school he modified his costume in the restroom, covered it with rips and nasty slogans and fake blood. I gave a snort of a laugh, thinking about that, and when I looked up, everybody was staring at me with the same strange expression on their faces.

I clasped my hands, leaned forward, and looked down at the floor, waiting for Officer Stephens to ask something else. There was a little green caterpillar down there, curled up tight into a spiral. A spiral much like the ones in the black dog's eyes, except that those spirals whirled. Steve had a spiral tattoo on his ankle, and we stayed up half of one night in Zero's funky little backyard talking about why he'd got it and what it . . .

"Was there drinking involved?" Officer Stephens asked.

I shrugged but didn't look up. "Beer." After a while I added, "Because it was the last bonfire of the season."

Why would they send my old DARE officer to do this? If they thought they were doing me a favor because Officer Stephens had a reputation for relating to kids, well, they weren't. He was the last person I wanted to talk to about the convenience store, the borrowed ID and the two wrapped packages, the zinc mine fields. Why should I explain to him that there was beer at the bonfires each and every time? Let Officer Stephens and the rest of them think what they thought. What difference could it possibly make now?

He asked a few other things and I stared at the spiral caterpillar and said what I said, I really can't remember what that was. Then finally he asked a wrap-up question. "Can you remember the last thing the driver, Treyston Hughes, said to you?"

"No," I answered. It was *don't you dare puke in my car,* but there's no way I would have told Officer Stephens or anybody else that. It was mine, those words. It was *ours.*

It wouldn't have sounded friendly or natural if it hadn't been us saying it and hearing it.

I was so glad to get out of that small green room. It smelled like flop sweat, like the kind of sweat people sweat when they're stringing together lies.

It was nearly 2 a.m. when we got in the Taurus and Janet started driving us home. She had a bit of trouble because the chamber of commerce always strings a dense web of small orange lights in the shape of jack-o'-lanterns across Main Street in late October.

"All this light clutter drives me absolutely nuts," she complained in a hollow voice that didn't sound the slightest bit like her voice. "I can't for the life of me see how people pick out which are the regular old stoplights in time to stop."

By then she'd run one red light and had slammed on the brakes just in time to stop at the one where we were then stopped. From the corner of my eye I saw she had a shaky death grip on the steering wheel. She wasn't looking at me and I wasn't looking at her. She hadn't even asked about my police sweatpants or about the yellow sack in my lap.

"They shouldn't have got you out so late," I murmured. "I coulda handled it myself."

The light turned green, but Janet didn't seem interested.

"I'm so heartsick for you, Tuck," she whispered. "And I'm so heartsick for dear little Trey, and for those other young boys."

"Light's green," I mentioned, though it was by then yellow, going on red again.

She turned off the car and sat holding her own arms, looking straight ahead. The light had turned red and now turned green again. I glanced over my shoulder and saw a lone pickup truck behind us. After a while the driver gave a single, polite honk.

Janet hit her own horn fiercely several times with her balled-up fist. The truck drove meekly around us and on down the deserted, glowing street. The driver even touched the brim of his Stetson as he passed, offering a sort of cowboy apology.

"Tucker, I know you must surely be in shock like the police were saying, but you better be listening up anyhow," Janet said in a sharp whisper. I looked over and she caught me by the wrist. Her eyes were bright and so crazy I didn't dare pull away.

"You have no idea how bad you look, Tucker, and why wouldn't you look bad? What just happened is the worst that could happen. Unless you'd lost a child, that is, which'd be far, far worse, the *very* worst that could happen to anyone, hands down."

I tried to ease from her grip, and she shook her head and threw my hand back to me.

"Do you remember when my dad and I moved in with you and your dad, Tuck?" she demanded. "Huh? Do you remember? Oh, Tucker, you were only eight and your mama had died just two years before. Your dad hadn't even kept a picture of her."

Red pain had begun ripping through my legs. I focused on it and turned to stare out my window.

"So I went to the public library and found one in the 1994 Clevesdale High yearbook, her senior picture. I made a pretty good copy, good as they could do at the Kinko's in Tulsa, and I framed it up and hung it down low where you could see it."

I drew a circle in the condensation my breath was leaving on the window. I touched a point in the middle and began drawing a wobbly spiral out from it. The whole thing melted into a mess before I'd got it done.

"Your father was *so* unknowable," she said in an angry mutter. "I couldn't pry that man open for love or money. When he got laid off from his job he just up and walked away, just disappeared on us, and I believe that was because he never learned to open up and share himself with anyone. And the worst thing? I doubt he realizes how much he lost when he lost us, because he never let *that* kind of knowledge in, either."

She made a sort of choked sound, then grabbed my wrist again and dug in with her fingernails. My skin felt tight all over, like it was shrinking. I wanted out of my skin, my bones. My body was a sack of suffocating pain and I couldn't breathe inside it.

"And Tucker, I don't like saying it, but you can be *so* much like him. I'm talking about how you acted back there in the station. And how you're acting right now. Don't you use the excuse of some Quapaw silence to go missing on me just like he did, you hear? Because it'd just kill me, it really would."

I pulled in some air. "Light's green," I told her.

"Do you think I give one single damn what color that damn light is?" She snatched the yellow bag from my hands and slammed herself sideways so hard against her door that it flew open, then rocked on its hinges. She ran from the car, stumbled over the curb, but recovered her balance and ran on to stuff the yellow sack viciously into the wire mesh trash receptacle chained in front of Andersen's Good Value Pharmacy.

I'd never heard Janet say "damn" before. But it was nothing if not a night of firsts.

She ran back and dropped into her seat, then just stared at me again with such fierceness that I had to keep my head somewhat turned toward her.

"I'm taking you to the clinic tomorrow to get those legs treated, mister, and I don't want one single little word of argument about it, you hear me?" She turned the key and gave the car about a gallon of gas and we lurched through the most recent red light.

"Better close your door," I quietly advised, and she noticed it was open and closed it.

IV

WHEN WE GOT HOME, I drug upstairs, took faux-hawked Larry's painkillers from my sweatshirt pocket and flushed them down the toilet, then went into my room and dropped onto my bed. The backs of the police sweatpants had molded themselves to my legs and were plastered there with blood, but I didn't have the energy to peel them off. Besides, the pain might lessen if they were off, and I'd decided that red pain was the only real thing I had to hang on to. Without it I'd fall right off the world and into a bottomless pit as black as the monster dog I couldn't possibly have seen but did see anyway.

I closed my eyes and saw Trey's hectic last dance against my lids. I sat up, panting, and rubbed hard at my face, then I eased myself back to stare bleakly at the ceiling shadows. I envied the mindless nothingness of those shadows. I wanted to *be* them.

The shadows suddenly moved together and turned into a spiral, a lopsided and innocent-looking spiral like a child would have drawn, just like the one on Steve's ankle.

Steve hadn't wanted to go to England to visit his dad last

summer, but his mother insisted. "It'll get you out of my hair," Steve said she said. When she found out it would cost his dad a lot more, she even let Steve take his guitar and clarinet. I guess Steve's good looks translate well because he came back from his month over there with love bites thick on his neck and with that small spiral tat.

We met him at the Tulsa airport in the Mustang and had a welcome home barbecue for him that night. By then we'd been barbecuing in Zero's backyard a couple of times a month for well over a year, ever since Steve taught us the joys of doing it. I was our official cook. Burgers, hot dogs, and baby back ribs, our splurge meal. They were easy to please. They liked their meat raw, medium, or burned.

Since I've worked several summers at Greenfield's Landscaping, I've gotten way into gardening. I even set up a hoop house in our backyard a couple of years ago, twelve by eight. It's a greenhouse made of clear plastic stretched over 16-foot iron rods that are bent into semi-circles then stuck deep into the ground. I put together extravagant salads for those barbecues. They raved about my cooking.

Besides the moon, the only illumination in Zero's bathroom-sized backyard was the many strings of colored lights his mother had twisted through the branches of the two large mimosa trees, saying it reminded her of her girlhood in Haiti. Those barbecues were why I started keeping my small flashlight on my belt, for enough light to cook by. Zero's mother thought flashlights caused brain damage and wouldn't keep one around.

Zero's second cousin Maxwell went to prison a few years ago and left behind his two huge brown velvet sofas, so those were the seating. They'd deteriorated about as much as they could, so we didn't have to be careful with our food, which was good, dark as it is back there. The sofas face each other with maybe three feet of walk space between them. They're a little or a lot damp, depending on how recently it's rained or snowed.

The night that Steve got back, he and Zero took one sofa and faced each other like mirror images, one knee up, one elbow over the back of the sofa, both rapt in eager conversation about England. Trey put in a word from the other sofa once in a while, but he was busy texting back and forth with this girl he was dating from somewhere in Texas. He'd met her when he and his band played in her town, and he'd only seen her once in the six months since. But until he gave up on owning a phone, he texted girls he'd met on the road like that a lot, sometimes juggling two or three girls in the same night.

I stood behind the grill and savored all of it, the August heat loosening its grip, the sickening-sweet smell of mimosa, the breeze that rocked those dozens of pinpoint lights, my friends' overlapping voices and opinions, their different ways of laughing. Zero hooted or snorted, Trey gave a sort of guttural giggle, and Steve usually confined his mirth to a polite twitter but was capable of an all-out series of honks that was hilarious.

"Do they surf?" Zero mostly wanted to know about England. He'd surfed a few times at his aunt's condo in Florida, and he dreamed of doing a lot more of it. "It's a small country with water on all sides, so you could get to a beach quick from anywhere."

Steve didn't know much about that, except that the water was cold, he thought. "Blues clubs are few and far between in Wiltshire, which is the part of England where my dad is," he complained. "And stuff is too tidy, you know? Like in a book or something, all dolled up." He looked around Zero's yard and nodded appreciatively. Clearly, in Steve's opinion at least, England suffered by comparison.

"They're cutting edge where alternative music's concerned, have been since the Rolling Stones," Trey put in distractedly, frowning at the message on his phone.

I turned the ribs, plastering them again with sauce. Now that it was almost completely dark, from where I stood, I could only make out certain parts of each of my friends, the parts I would know them anywhere by. Trey's bright hair falling in his face as his thumbs moved delicately and fast on his lighted phone, Steve's length and graceful slouch, and the way Zero's plans and ideas kept his feet and fingers and dreads in slight motion that stirred the gathering darkness.

"What's with the spiral on your ankle?" Zero asked Steve.

It was the question we'd been waiting for, and things went instantly quiet. The story of that tattoo was going to be good, probably some situation with an English girl.

Steve straightened and stretched. Then, "Okay, guys, you gotta promise you'll believe me because I don't believe myself, but I gotta because I *saw* it with my eyes." He pointed to his eyes with his index fingers, illustrating.

Trey pocketed his phone. I put my barbecue fork down on the broken air conditioner that served as my cook's table and went to get comfortable on Trey's half-empty sofa.

Steve sat forward, pushed his light hair behind his ears, then braced his elbows on his legs and let his long, callused fingers dangle, frowning in thought.

"Well, I got bored, see," Steve began, "and my dad didn't want me moping around, not when he's got this new wife to show off for, so he gives in and rents me a motorbike. You would not believe some of those English bikers, guys! They go right down the middle of the road, use the broken highway line as their own special track!"

Trey and I glanced at Zero, who sure enough had that open-mouthed, dazzled look on his face that meant he'd be trying some variation of that crazy little trick real soon.

"So one day I was toodling on that bike and ended up in this town called Avesbury. It was cool. It's got a stone circle running right through it. Like Stonehenge. Only their stones are more spread out. And I found a decent pub there too, with fair music. Pub food is gross, decent or not, but there were friendly people drinking and they told me I should stop on the way home at this hill that's actually an ancient cone-shaped pyramid or something. And a girl I was chatting with said there's also an ancient burial ground not far from that hill, a thing called a barrel.

"This girl went on to say she'd be too scared at that barrel place when it was almost dark and that I should spend the night with her and her roommate and we'd all three go out there in the morning, but who'd want to go to a place like that in full daylight? Twilight was edging in, and by the time I got there, it would be perfect, was my thinking."

He paused to see if we were following along, and we nodded in an interested way, probably listening to his story less than wondering why Steve had all the luck with girls and so often squandered it.

"Okay, so I get back on the bike and start toward home. Well, I'd noticed all these huge wheat fields when I'd been riding out earlier, and now all of a sudden I'm just riding along when ka-*bam!*" He slapped his leg so hard some dirt flew from the sofa. "There's a hu*mong*ous crop circle there in the middle of one of those fields, and I would *swear* it had not been there when I'd passed it before! I mean, boys, I'm talking a circle big as a basketball court all filled up with whirls and hexagons and lots and lots of spirals." He pointed to his new tattoo, in case we didn't get it. "Like *this.*

"So I pull my motorbike into this little stopping place they have beside their roads, they call them lay-its or lay-outs or something. Lay-bys. And I'm looking at the circle from that lay-by when I notice a small brown sign on the fence that reads *West Kennet Long Barrow* with an arrow pointing to this little path right along the left edge of that wheat. And I think a minute, did that girl at the pub say maybe 'barrow' instead of 'barrel'? Hey, I could very well visit an ancient burial site right up against a genuine crop circle, and all of this just as the sun sets, how cool would that be?"

Steve scanned our faces, waiting for an answer from us each.

"Very cool," Zero told him in an awed whisper.

"Plenty cool," Trey allowed, shaking his hair from his face.

I nodded in agreement, then whispered, "Hold on one second." I rushed over to turn my ribs, slathering them with sauce for a final time.

When I got back, Steve was stretched out with his hands behind his head and his boots crossed at the ankles. "That smells so freakin' good, Tuck. Let's eat."

"No! Back to the burial site," Zero ordered. "C'mon, did you see anything or not?"

Trey snickered and wriggled his fingers. "Little green men, riding on the shoulders of little green men?"

"Well, laugh if you want," Steve said solemnly, "but I tell you, as I walked that path to that barrow place, my hair stood on end. Every single hair on my head just suddenly stood at attention, not from fear but from some force I reckon was coming from that crop circle. I kid you not, boys, there was something out there, some force.

"And when I finally reached that amazing rock tomb, it had a strong feeling of something still being there, after all this time. I mean, some ancient sadness, or maybe some ancient magic? It was empty, sure, but not all that deserted, not from the feel of it. No skeletons now, but I guess the whole place was filled at one time with bones. And the tomb's marked on the outside and on the inside with, guess what? Spirals. Someone ancient has carved out spirals on some of those huge rocks, just like someone or something not so ancient carved them in that wheat. So. Let's get at that barbecue."

We laughed at Steve's sudden hunger-driven change of subject, but in a serious enough way to let him know we believed him. Then we got up and got set to eat, figuring that was it, the end of the story of his spiral tat.

But after we'd finished our ribs and were licking our fingers and slouching on the sofas, too full to move or even to talk much, Zero sleepily asked Steve, "So did you ever come upon that cone-shaped pyramid thing that girl in the pub told you about?"

"Oh, for sure I did," Steve answered. "I forgot to tell you, when I was walking back along that path, I saw a thing like a big upside-down cone looming there right pretty much across the road from where I'd left the bike. I guess I'd missed it before 'cause I'd only had eyes for that circle, but seeing it on the way back from that barrow, I knew right away it was that ancient structure, that Silbury Hill she'd mentioned, what else could it be?

"And when I'd reached the bike, there was just enough light for me to see across the road and, well, there was maybe a hundred big old rabbits standing on different parts of that cone-hill, not one of them moving a single muscle. I started the bike and none of them twitched a twitch at the loud sound of it. Every single one of them faced the same direction, too—east, not a west-facer in the crowd. They seemed under some witchy spell or something. I hung around another couple of minutes, and when *still* nobody moved, well, I couldn't get out of there fast enough. And the next day I got me this tattoo to remind me of seeing a hundred frozen rabbits all up and down a pyramid hill." He murmured, "I coulda got a rabbit tat, but I just knew whatever was going on with them had to do with those spirals on those burial rocks and inside that big old crop circle."

Something passed among the other three of us. Before, his story had been interesting, but we all knew a little bit about crop circle pranksters and static electricity that could play with your hair. My hair, for instance, had gone straight up when I was on a scouting camp-out on a mountain in Colorado right before a thunderstorm hit. Steve was so . . . something, romantic? A southern boy from Memphis, he swore he'd seen Elvis's ghost at least four times, so what he saw with his own eyes was a bit suspect.

But who would imagine a hill of frozen rabbits? Unlike Elvis, rabbits were ordinary and simple. What other ordinary things might go all spooky at any minute?

"If one small impossible thing happens, that makes *anything* possible," Zero finally said, putting into words what I myself had been thinking. His voice had that awed, breathless tone typical of him when he was caught up in the beauty of science or planning something crazy.

I remember wanting to turn my flashlight on or to go somewhere light.

"There are spirals in the Nazca lines in Peru," I said, remembering a report I'd done. "I think other ancient Indian cultures used them in their sacred rites as well."

"You start at the outside and spiral into the heart of a good piece of music," Trey mused. "Any good beat does that, leads you inward toward the beat of your own heart."

Zero disagreed. "Nah, a spiral's gotta lead *out*! You start at the center and journey outward, gaining constant acceleration until you reach the rim and go *airborne,* dudes!"

Zero bounced to a crouch there on the grungy sofa, then took another bounce, propelling himself up onto the sofa's sagging back. He assumed a skateboarder's position against the rising moon, wrangling the darkness with both outspread arms and all the muscled will in the world while Trey and I slid to make a place for Steve to sit and finish his third ear of corn.

If one small impossible thing happens, that makes anything possible.

My eyes came open with a start and I saw that the shadow spiral on my bedroom ceiling had been replaced with weak, flickering daylight. I'd slept some after all and now it was morning, Sunday, which meant it was Janet's busiest day at Bob's Family Restaurant. She would have left at six. My digital clock said 6:37. She'd be gone.

A feeling of overwhelming doom was coming awake along with me. I tried to hold it back, tried not to let it swamp me. But toxic images from last night came pouring like acid into my head, destroying all sense, all reality. I pulled my pillow over my face and concentrated on sending all my attention to the burning in my legs.

They felt turned inside out. It was an ordeal getting up. My knees would barely bend, and the sheet beneath me was bloodied, a real mess that I couldn't let Janet see. I hobbled into the bathroom, got into the shower, and watched blood and mud mix at my feet and swirl down the drain. I pushed my hands and forearms hard against the shower wall, but still I heard myself moan. I hobbled back into my room and dressed in a T-shirt and jeans, biting my bottom lip bloody as I pulled that rough denim up over all that skinless flesh.

The phone kept ringing and ringing, the one downstairs. I'd turned off my own phone yesterday, hoping to get some studying done before the bonfire. Now I took it from the backpack on my desk and saw it was clogged with messages. I frowned at it, then bent, stifling a groan, and threw it under the bed. I heard it skid into a nest of books and shoes, out of my reach and sight.

Janet's father, Bud, was still snoring across the hall, which was good. Since we shared the bathroom, I'd been worried I'd wake him before I could figure out how to dodge him. The last thing I wanted was to have to talk to anyone, and it was especially hard to talk to Bud these days, he was so old. I stripped the bed and took the long and painful journey down the stairs. I shuffled to the laundry nook, stuffed my sheets into the washing machine, dumped Tide and half a gallon of Clorox in with them, slammed the lid, and started the machine. Then I shuffled aimlessly back into the kitchen.

There was the usual note from Janet tacked with one of her heart-shaped magnets on the refrigerator, written Saturday night before she went to bed, giving me Sunday morning instructions and late-breaking Saturday news and so forth.

Tuck—Just thought you should know Bud made me take him for his driver's test again this afternoon and, no big surprise, he failed. The eye test part, like both other times. They won't let him take it a fourth time, so he'll be grouchy tomorrow when he gets up. Just thought you ought to be warned. xxoo Janet PS Don't show this to Bud!

Good old Janet, always leaving a *PS* to warn you of something obvious. She'd written this, what? Three hours before she got the midnight police call? I stared at the bright yellow bee printed in the corner of her notepaper. The smile of the identical bees on each sheet of Janet's notepaper was not just insane like I'd always thought but completely sinister, I saw now. It mocked those who actually had to somehow live, not just pretend to, who actually had to deal second by second with three dangerous dimensions. I wanted to tear off that bee's paper legs, to make it suffer, because suffering was another thing it knew absolutely nothing about and never would.

I crumpled the paper and tossed it hard into the waste bin, then wandered out the back door from force of habit, heading vaguely to the hoop house like I did all mornings. The dew crawled up my jeans, clammy and cold against my throbbing legs.

Things inside the little greenhouse were so lush. Arugula, chard, all those good salad fixings. This would have been a perfect barbecue day, cool and sunny.

I began to shake, hard, all over. I fumbled for some of the vegetables nearest my feet and rolled them into my shirt, then I lumbered back inside, dumped the bright, strobing vegetables onto the table, and stared at them, trying to remember what they were.

The phone in the kitchen started ringing again. I picked it up before I remembered I didn't want to. It was Mary Beth Chandler. Under other circumstances, I would have considered a call from her an answered prayer. Any boy in the junior class would have.

"Dead," she whispered into my ear. "Zero, Trey, Steve, all dead. It's just so unbelievable, Tucker, you know? And we figured you were with them last night . . . before? So Jessie and Aimee are here with me. We had a sleepover after the, well, after the bonfire was, you know, called off because of, well, you know. And we're calling to tell you we're, like, really, really sorry. But glad it wasn't you too, I mean. Oh, Tuck! This is just so awful, you know? Well, of course you do, you guys were best friends."

"Right." I knew all three things she'd mentioned. It was unbelievable, and it was awful. And we were best friends. Zero and then Steve ever since they moved to Clevesdale, but Trey and I practically forever, since we were barely four years old.

At first I hated Wee Ones Preschool because this kid named Charley kept hitting me on the head day after day with a can of chicken noodle soup he'd pilfered from somewhere and kept hidden in his Spider-Man backpack. Then suddenly this boy with crazy orange hair arrived for the first time, teary-eyed from being left behind by his mother. I told him a story to make him feel better, the one my own mother had told me the day she first left me there, something about a bulldozer named Annie who loved doing preschool things, sharing crayons, making music. By the end of that story our friendship was sealed, and the very next day Trey saved me from Charley.

He tricked Charley into taking off his right shoe by telling him there was a rock in it, then he threatened to have a Ninja Turtle action figure bite off Charley's big toe unless Charley gave up that can of soup. I can still see four-year-old Trey kneeling, his hair a bright tangled curtain on both sides of his face as he held that action figure so close to Charley's bare foot that Charley didn't dare move or even scream for grown-up help. Trey calmly waited for Charley to quit his angry but silent crying and to simply surrender his unlawful weapon, and Charley finally threw the can of soup at the wall and a girl named Jessica pounced on it and took it home in her Barbie case that afternoon.

Everyone was so impressed by the clever bravado behind that plan that Trey pretty much took over leadership of the rug-rat societal structure at Wee Ones. We all began letting him decide complicated things—how long someone's block tower had to stand before someone else could charge over and knock it down, what you could cut when we got to use scissors and what it wasn't cool to cut even if the teacher wasn't looking, how many people it took to cram the ragtag stuffed animals back into their tattered refrigerator box at day's end.

Over and over again I saw Trey gain that same sort of respect in various situations. He was the renegade trickster rabbit that people wanted to win the costume contest, not because he was bad in a cool way or even because his costume was good in a gross way but because he was unpredictable and fun-loving and patient with his plans. Trey never settled for smiling if the flashier response of howling was what the occasion called for.

He was fond of risks because they made his life exciting and paid off for him far more often than they didn't, and he was lucky and well liked. And I was his friend and became entitled through his friendship to the other two good friends Trey picked up along the way, guys similarly flashy and lucky and risky. Zero in eighth grade, Steve in ninth.

"Tucker? Hey, are you still there?"

"Right."

"So, Jess and Aimee and I are making black armbands, enough for everybody. Out of, like, respect? To wear at school and stuff. We'll give them to the juniors tomorrow, and the senior cheerleaders will give them to the seniors. Because see, Jilly and Kim and Traci are making them too. It was Traci's idea. We wanted you to know. It's the least we can do. What . . . was it like, Tuck? Awful, right?"

A large black ant was traveling across the windowsill, dragging a crumb behind him. The ant was acting like the whole future of the world hung on what it was doing with that probably moldy piece of something. At any second I could drop on it with my fist and crumbs or anything else would have absolutely no meaning for it any longer.

"Tucker?"

"Mary Beth, did you see a large black dog at the bonfire? Or . . . or on the bluff road?" I swallowed. "A sort of . . . well, *deformed* dog, in the air, like, flying?"

A few beats of silence. "Tucker, I know you're messed up, but that's not funny. And I'm supposed to ask you, for Lily, if Steve was going to ask her to the dance next week, because Tonya said he had already asked *her* and Lily's so upset that she's just hysterical because she feels Tonya is just a liar because how could she prove it, and—"

I hung up the phone, though I wasn't sure Mary Beth had finished talking. Now the ant was climbing vertically up the window. It went behind the curtain, so I tore the curtain down and kicked it out of the way. The ant was still dragging that precious crumb, but at my slightest whim the crumb would disintegrate into microscopic crumbs of a crumb and the ant would become just a shiny blotch of shapeless black. Its friends at the anthill would never have any idea what had become of—

"What happened to Janet's little blue curtain?"

I jerked up and turned, my heart slamming. "G'morning, Bud."

He was standing in the kitchen doorway, wearing his usual gray pants and white shirt, but he was barefoot, which was very, very strange. I couldn't remember ever seeing him barefoot, without his brown nylon socks and shiny brown dress shoes or at least his leather slippers. The hairs on his toes were as black as the hair on my own head, though Bud's few head hairs had been white for as long as I'd known him.

"Right, Bud. Uh, I guess it fell." I tried not to yelp as I bent to retrieve the curtain. When I had the thing hanging again, I took some stiff, calculated steps toward the doorway, hoping to somehow ease past Bud and get on up to my room. Bud journeyed to a place—a doorway, the bathroom, the narrow lane between the table and refrigerator—then just stood there and was basically unmovable. He was built like a tree trunk, wide across the shoulders, waist, and hips. He was basically rooted wherever he stood.

He raised a hand to stop me, then took the other hand from behind his back. "I believe you left these in the bathroom."

From his big, blunt fingers dangled the police sweatpants. He gave them a little shake, and dark clots of hardened blood fell like sleet onto the kitchen linoleum.

V

I WATCHED MY ARM reach for the blood-encrusted pants. "Thanks," I croaked.

I gripped one leg, but Bud held on to the other and pulled me a step closer to him with it. "Korea," he said grimly and quietly. "Thirty-eighth Parallel. I saw some things. They burn a tattoo right onto your soul. Try losing it. You can't!"

My throat went dry. "Who . . . who burns a tattoo, Bud?" I pushed out.

"When Janet got a call from the police last night, I turned on my radio. Three boys killed in a car and one injured. I'm guessing from the look of these pants and the police call that you were that fourth boy, am I correct? And that the others were those three boys you've brought to the house now and then."

I took a long, shuddering breath. "I got out of the car and they drove on."

Bud didn't reply to that, just nodded and let go of his leg of the police pants. He began his usual slow morning trek through the kitchen to the refrigerator. He pried the refrigerator door open and stood eyeing the empty egg container, shaking his head. It was no secret that Bud thought Janet should be home, buying eggs, talking to him, and being happy. For some reason Bud's look of egg despair hit me hard, though, and my stomach began to feel all knotted and strange. I needed something, maybe orange juice.

"We've got Pop-Tarts," I told Bud as I eased past him and headed to the toaster.

Bud turned from the refrigerator to his chair and dropped into it with an exhausted groan. His toenails looked like hooves, thick and yellow, curving inward over his toes.

While the Pop-Tarts cooked, I got out the orange juice and two glasses.

"So, the police picked you up on the bluff road, drove you down to the beach, and called Janet to meet you there and bring you home?"

Even two-handed I couldn't make the juice hit our glasses more than the counter. The toaster made the trampoline sound it makes when the Pop-Tarts are done.

"Something like that." I groped for a subject change. "Aren't your feet cold?"

"Nah. I got no feeling in them since this last heart event. *You're* walking like your legs are wood. I'm guessing that's where your worst injuries occurred, in your leg area."

I got the Pop-Tarts and put them on a couple of saucers for us. Neither of us made a move to eat ours, though. I can't speak for Bud, but mine just didn't seem appetizing. I don't know what can go wrong with a simple Pop-Tart, but it seemed off. Made of something like plastic foam, or flesh.

"Janet should get those Hungry Jack biscuits again," Bud grumbled.

I stared at my plate and muttered, "She wants to take me to the doctor this afternoon."

"Well, don't let them give you a cockamamie eye test," Bud muttered back. "I been driving without a bit of trouble since I was fourteen years old!"

"Right, no eye test," I assured him, then I took a deep breath and pushed myself up to a stand. I gathered our plates and glasses and began the long, painful walk to the sink.

"Dead friends," Bud said quietly behind me, then sighed a long, rickety sigh. "Lucky you didn't see yours that way. Dead, I mean. The sight burns a tattoo right into your soul. Shut your eyes and there they are, against your lids. Or you'll look at an empty sky and it'll suddenly fill with the sight."

I decided rinsing our stuff could wait, and I clattered the plates and glasses into the sink. "Later, Bud," I threw over my shoulder, then I got out of the kitchen.

The trek upward was agonizing, much worse than coming down had been. You never think about it, but climbing stairs absolutely requires bendable knees.

Once inside my room, I pushed the door closed and leaned back against it. I stared at nothing for a while, then I covered my eyes with my hands and, just like Bud had said, the thing started replaying itself against my lids, Trey behind that wheel,

Trey when that smoke had lightened for that second, Trey doing his fire-fueled crazy dance. That rubber tarp blowing off Zero for a second before faux-hawked Larry tacked it back down.

I began a wooden-legged sort of clumsy pacing, huffing in little bits of air without exhaling. I'd forgotten *how* to exhale, how to do the simple act of breathing! I got dizzy, light-headed, but all I could think about was keeping my eyes stretched wide open.

And then, a handful of rocks suddenly hit my bedroom window, the sort of small hard-thrown pebbles Trey was always picking up from the little kids' play area at the park behind his house and saving in a coffee can in the Mustang for when he needed my attention in the middle of the night.

No one but Trey ever threw rocks against my window. No one.

I froze for maybe five seconds, completely froze, then I ordered my burning legs to move and I charged to that window and looked out, my fingers splayed against the glass. Was I longing for it to be Trey? Trey back from wherever? Ghostly Trey, skeletal and charred Trey? I could see our whole block of small houses, and there was nobody around. The trees in the yards of our subdivision are small and scrubby ones, and no one, not even a tiny child, could hide behind one of them. There was nothing out there.

But caught on the window ledge, still teetering, was one of Trey's brown pebbles.

Breathe, I told myself. *Breathe!* Things were going black around the edges, but in the nick of time I grabbed a deep gulp of air, my head cleared a bit, and then, I saw it.

Near the McKees' mailbox, almost directly across the street.

The dog. It was working at the ground with its tremendous forefeet, digging exactly where I myself had stood just yesterday afternoon when Trey had ordered me to drive. Then it stuck its middle head into the hole it had made and came up with a small bright green something in its mouth.

So there it was, in broad daylight. With its middle head it looked proudly up at me with that green thing in its mouth as though it expected some kind of reward. Meanwhile its left head was turned to gaze down Cottonwood Street in the direction of Best Buy. Its right head stared with great interest at the long string of something that looked like moldy sausage hanging out of one of the overflowing garbage cans in the McKees' side yard.

I could see a dizzy sort of movement in its eyes that was those spooky spirals.

I pushed off from the window, then stumbled through my room, knocking over a chair, slip-sliding on clothes. I exploded out the door and into the hallway. I bounced stiff-legged down the stairs three at a time and staggered through the den.

Bud was snoring in his La-Z-Boy recliner, and when I passed, I yelled, "Bud, there's something you gotta see, right across the street! Hurry!"

Gruff and grouchy Bud, who could be a better witness? People would believe him because he never bothered to lie. And if Bud saw no three-headed dog? "You're crazy, kid," Bud would say, and he'd be right. Either way, I had to know.

"Whassit? wha . . . ?" Bud sat up, then pushed himself to a

wobbly stand, disoriented but game. "Go ahead!" He waved a hand. "I'm right behind you."

I jerked open the front door and ran across the porch, but I could already see that the dog was gone. I jumped the porch stairs and did a bouncing jog across the street. There wasn't even a hole in the McKees' yard to show where the mutt had been digging.

But when I got right to the spot where the dog had been, I saw Trey's cheap little bright green Bic cigarette lighter lying in the brown grass. I grabbed it and stashed it in my pocket before it too could disappear, then I loped stiffly back to where Bud was framed in the open doorway of the house.

"There was a dog over there a minute ago," I called to Bud.

Bud frowned. "So? What's the big deal about a dog?"

"It looked a lot like our old Lab, Ringo." Except for a few huge details.

We heard Janet's muffler in the near distance and turned to watch the Taurus swaying slowly down the middle of the street.

"She left work awful early for a Sunday, way before the Baptist rush," Bud observed. "I expect she got to thinking she didn't want to wait until afternoon to get you to the clinic." He snorted and muttered, "She's big on hauling people to that clinic."

The pain came surging back, worse than ever. It had taken a brief vacation while my brain used all its energy to try and figure out the deal with that dog. But now the red throbbing returned and I welcomed it, the only real thing I had now that everything else was disintegrating into senselessness.

I pushed my hand deep inside my pocket and gripped the lighter. "I don't want the clinic messing with me," I heard myself murmur darkly. "I *need* this pain."

"I read you loud and clear, kid," Bud totally shocked me by responding. And then he came slowly down the porch stairs and walked in his stiff-backed way clear down the sidewalk to stand rooted near the garage.

Janet maneuvered right over the curb and into the driveway. She gave us both a tired smile as she threw her shoulder against her door and got out.

"There are a couple sacks of groceries in the trunk, Tuck." She bent to gather her purse and waitressing uniform. "Dad, I got you some of those breakfast biscuits you've been wanting."

I took the keys from the ignition and walked back to the trunk.

"Janet, a man's wounds are his own," I heard Bud tell her. "This guy doesn't want to go to the clinic, so don't pester him about it and that's that!"

Bud never talked to Janet like that. Never. I stayed hidden behind the open lid of the trunk. Janet said nothing, and a couple of minutes later I saw Bud walking back toward the porch in a proud way, putting all his weight on one foot at a time, holding his arms out from his body for balance.

I finally hung both grocery sacks from my left wrist and slammed the trunk closed.

Janet was looking straight at me with tears in her eyes. "I just don't want to take any chances with you, Tuck," she said in a ragged whisper.

But that ship had sailed. All the chances had already been taken as of last night. She didn't get that, but Bud did, from Korea.

I twisted my mouth into a reassuring smile. "My legs feel a hundred percent better. Once I showered, they turned out to be barely scratched."

I went on inside with those groceries, thinking how I owed Bud a huge one.

The rest of Sunday afternoon I stayed up in my room, lying on the bed and flicking Trey's lighter. Ringo lay there next to me with his head on my chest, comforting me with his terrible, familiar breath. He's so old that he usually doesn't climb the stairs, but that afternoon he somehow knew how much I needed him and made an effort.

I listened close in case more pebbles hit my window, but they didn't.

One time I heard Bud and Janet arguing and drifted out to the hall to eavesdrop, thinking it would be about the clinic and my legs. It turned out to be about Bud, though. Apparently the eye test people weren't the only ones giving him grief. His heart doctor wanted his driver's license taken away from him as well.

"But Dad, you *know* that Dr. Hitchford said if you had another heart attack and lost consciousness, it would be tragic if you were behind the wheel and—"

"I get a sorta warning before I pass out, Janet! I'd have *plenty* of time to pull over! What's Dr. Hitchford know about bum hearts anyhow, him barely forty years old?"

"Well, Dad, he *is* a cardiologist," Janet said meekly.

I went back to my room shaking my head, wishing there was some way I could trade places with Bud. He wanted to drive more than anything in the world, and the idea of driving made me sick to my stomach, as sick as when I'd bailed from Trey's car and thrown up in the ditch. I would never drive again. That hadn't been a hard decision, hadn't even taken any actual thought. It was just a fact. Driving a car had slipped quietly and firmly all by itself onto the list of things I was never going to do, like eating live scorpions, or cutting off one of my ears, or sticking my hand into boiling tar.

After we ate that night, Janet went back to the restaurant to help close up. I was sitting in the den with Bud when the phone rang. It was Aimee, the cheerleader who'd dated Zero for a couple of weeks in September, then had dropped him flat and more or less broken his heart for about a day and a half.

"Tucker?" She was crying. "Listen, Zero gave me a white rose corsage for the dance last month, did . . . did you know that?"

"No." She must have ordered Zero to buy her that. You had to tell Zero everything where the everyday world was concerned. His head was filled with velocities and angles and variable resistances. There was little room left for things like flowers.

I began watching Bud for something to do while Aimee talked. He was staring glassy-eyed at a really, really old VCR tape of a Monday night football game. The Chiefs were playing. Joe Montana was going long, long. . . .

"Pure white roses were . . . were *our* flowers, Tuck. One day in study hall Zero kicked the back of my chair twelve times, and I turned around to glare at him and he just smiled back that goofy smile nobody could resist. Then that afternoon this florist arrived at my house with a huge box of . . . of twelve white roses. That's how we . . . started."

I'd bet anything Aimee ordered Zero to buy her *those* twelve roses too, probably as a fine for kicking her chair. I'm also guessing he didn't really think about there being the most beautiful girl in class in that chair when he got the urge to do a little resistance experiment using the back of the chair and the toe of his boot. I bet he was recording the amount of reverb each time he kicked, the number of centimeters his boot bounced back.

Zero's smile *was* lopsidedly goofy, but it went with his flashing eyes and his flowing mess of wild hair. Had Aimee dated Zero on a dare from her girlfriends? We wondered. But then again, Zero's confidence and his startling looks always seemed to work in his favor, at least at first. *I wanta ride the sky like I was an eagle!* Since he thought he could fly his skateboard down Hawk's Slope, he probably could have. Since he thought he could date Aimee, he could, for a little while. *How you do a tricky jump is you plot it out and think it, then right before you start, you don't think it. You know?*

"Interception!" Bud hollered, jerking his head back to show pure disgust at his team. Bud had seen this same play over and over again, so his reaction was not from mere surprise but rather from authentic, lasting shock that you had to respect. Almost instantly his mouth sagged open again and he went back to staring at the screen with no expression whatsoever except for a little dip of a frown in his thick, crazy eyebrows.

"So I called everyone on the student council and they agreed to buy some long-stemmed white roses for the funeral. Those of us who were closest to them will each carry a single white rose at the funeral, then at the end, we'll put them on the caskets as we file past as a gesture of . . . of—"

She broke off, sobbing, just as Bud's head flopped back against the headrest of the La-Z-Boy and he delivered a thundering prizewinner of a snore.

If Zero had been here, he would have been authentically impressed by that snore. Zero was democratic in his scientific enthusiasms. Outstanding body noises were worthy of his rapt attention just as much as geometric calculations were. He also adored stupid pet tricks, tornado-chasing, and kernoodling, catching giant catfish with your hand as bait.

". . . a gesture of . . ."

I hung up. I'd lost track of whether Aimee had finished talking, just like I'd lost track with Mary Beth early that morning. Aimee had mentioned Zero's smile, I was pretty sure of that much, but why bring it up since it was history now? Farewell to that goofy, lopsided smile and much of the rest of Zero's sharp, off-center, interesting face.

Bud had the remote somewhere, so I stood and walked to the television and turned the power off. Then I went down to a crouch there with my back braced by the TV screen. I wanted to simply watch Bud eye to eye for a minute, even though it would mean accepting the especially intense pain that crouching like that brought with it.

In contrast to everything else, Bud was nothing but real. His knees gaped wide. He'd left his slippers beside the chair, and his thin brown socks had a hole over each big toe. Bristly hairs grew like some sort of crop from the backs of his hands and from out of his large, red ears. The same sort of hairs curled in two bunches just beneath his nose, bending slightly upward as though seeking the light.

I waited for the remote to fall from the spot where it was delicately balanced on the chair arm, near Bud's elbow. I was willing to bet the clatter of that wouldn't quite wake Bud but would jerk the most amazing snore yet from him, a real record breaker.

And then my heart started doing a dance in my chest and I knew I was about to do something I shouldn't do, ever. I held my breath and swiveled around to crouch facing the dark screen of the TV. I gazed at my own reflection, with sleeping Bud murky in the background. I touched my eyes with two fingers, then I drew a straight line across my lips through the dust on the screen. Then I began to raise myself from my crouch slowly, slowly until the very top of my head disappeared, then most of the top of my hair disappeared, then my forehead began to disappear, and then all of my head was gone to just above my eyebrows. Gone! Just *gone*, like the brain part of Zero was . . . just *gone*, all that smartness just shredded into nothingness like a used-up pencil eraser.

"You and me should go see them Chiefs play."

I shot to my feet and whirled around. "Wow, Bud. You really scared me." My heart was acting like it'd come right through my rib cage and bounce around on the carpet. Had he seen, heard? "Yeah, maybe, sometime. I better get to bed. School tomorrow."

I tried to hurry out of the room, but my legs wouldn't do hurry. Some fledgling scabs had broken open when I'd crouched. If I wanted to move at all, it had to be in slow motion, one leg a few inches, the other a few inches.

"No time like the present. Now, this week. My treat. Hot dogs, the whole kaboodle."

I glanced at him and saw something in his eyes, some spark of something, nearly hidden by his grizzled mess of white eyebrows. Something that made me think he *had* seen what I was doing when I'd mimicked dead Zero, seen it and understood why I'd done it. But how *could* he understand something so shameful and crazy?

"Maybe. G'night, Bud." I felt like a spineless idiot. It wouldn't happen, going to a game, because neither of us could drive. He hadn't accepted the hard, cold fact that *he* couldn't drive and I couldn't begin to explain to him why *I* couldn't drive. I couldn't explain that to Bud or anybody else because I couldn't understand it myself.

VI

IT WAS A THRUMMING kind of quiet at school the next day. The kind of intense and unnatural quiet it would be if we were all in a play and Mr. Heggleston had given us stage directions. *Now, people, your friends died suddenly and tragically this past weekend. Act stunned. Act disbelieving. Cloak yourselves in layers of disbelief and horror, all right, people?* All day kids and teachers came up to me and said things I couldn't quite comprehend but I knew were sympathetic, put a quick hand on my shoulder as we passed in the hall, met my eyes, then gave me a heavyhearted look, things like that.

My last girlfriend, Alyssa, toodled her fingers at me in algebra, then looked very stricken and drew a tear down her cheek with her fingernail. I sort of waited for her outside the door after class, and she came up and took my arm. "I tried to call you. Several people are trying to call you, Tucker, but your *phone* isn't working."

It was an accusation. Alyssa is one of those people that feels not to have your phone always with you is criminal talk neglect. "I lost it," I lied.

Alyssa and I were probably never that good as a couple. She always wanted to know what I was thinking and was always telling me what she was thinking, which was usually that I wasn't telling her what I was thinking. But now she put her hand on my cheek, stood on tiptoe, and gave me a quick, friendly kiss. That was nice.

"You *call* me." She shoved me in the chest to bring home the urgency of that, then hurried on to her next class. If I called her, we'd only talk about why I hadn't called her before then, so I knew I wouldn't. Pain shot up my legs and I concentrated on it and let the hall surge move me along like a strong river current.

The cheerleaders gave out the armbands in a weepy, solemn way, and everyone wore theirs like a badge of something. Trapper Simkin, in his never-ending quest to be different, wore his around his leg, above his left knee, like a tourniquet. Aimee Stafleet wore a matching headband made from the same dull black cloth as the armbands.

After my third class, while I was at my locker staring at my stuff, our school counselor, Ms. Jazzmeyer, snuck up on me and clutched my shoulder. I whirled around to see her smiling sadly from beneath her short helmet of school-bus-colored hair.

"Tucker?" she said quietly, stroking my sleeve like it was a prize cat and not the ketchup-stained cuff of a track sweatshirt. I saw that her long fingernails were painted orange and black, the school colors, each one half and half.

"We're rounding up some really good people, grief counselors from Tulsa," she whispered, still petting my arm. "You just hang in there, sweetheart. They'll be here in the morning and you'll be first on our list. Okay, darlin'?" She gave my shoulder another squeeze.

"Okay," I answered, though I hadn't really comprehended a word she'd said. They'd hung in the air, those words, then crashed to the floor and splintered.

I saw my aching legs moving me down the halls the rest of the day, taking me to familiar places I would never have been able to find on my own. Occasionally I heard girls at their lockers talking in hushed voices about the upcoming funeral in much the same way they would have compared wardrobe notes before a basketball tournament.

"We'll all sit together and wear our armbands."

"Is everybody going to wear black anything else? Black skirts?"

"Black jeans? Are jeans even okay?"

"Wear waterproof mascara so you can cry," someone advised her friend in the exact same offhand way I myself had sometimes advised Trey to remember his sunglasses. *Wear your shades*, I was always telling him, because Trey kept them in the glove compartment of the Stang and usually forgot to take them out and put them on. *Sun'll be wicked at the game today. Better grab your shades.*

At the end of last period, Mr. Halen came on the intercom and said that classes would be dismissed at one fifteen the next afternoon so that students who desired to could attend the funeral. He cleared his throat. "Um, that is, funerals."

I mulled that over as I packed up my algebra book and followed my throbbing legs out the door. I couldn't decide. Did you say "funeral" or "funerals"? One service, three bodies. Did you say "desire" about something like going to see three kids buried?

Those vocabulary questions tricked off minor sparks in my brain as my legs led me to our neighborhood, but they didn't generate anything you could call actual thought.

Bud was sitting on the porch swing when I neared the house. He wasn't moving it, he was just sitting there straight and rigid like he always sits. A little slip of white skin showed above his socks and below the cuffs of his pants.

"Got my license for a quarter when I was fourteen years old and never had a bit of trouble on the highway," he called to me. "Learned at home on my dad's old pickup truck, back when they knew how to make a truck. Just turning the steering wheel of that big black Ford gave you automatic muscles."

"Hey, Bud," I greeted him.

"That truck and me was one unit, indivisible. Nobody could stop me drivin' if I was still in that 1936 Ford truck."

"Yeah, I know they wouldn't, Bud," I solemnly agreed. My throat felt husky. "You remember Trey, don't you? He felt exactly like that about his car."

You gotta see her, Graysten! Oh, dude, you have just gotta see her! I mean, she's rusting under a few other classic carcasses there at

Handerley's Salvage, but you gotta imagine her with about a dozen coats of cherry red paint and a classic speaker system. I was born to restore this '67 Stang! It's my calling in life, you know?

"He was one of the boys in that crash, right?" I nodded and Bud nodded along. Then we both were quiet for a minute. "Well. I believe she made lemon pie for dinner," he told me. It was his favorite. I appreciated him trying to cheer me up.

"I think I forgot to bring in vegetables this morning. Later, Bud."

I went around to the backyard. When I ducked through the plastic flap of the hoop house, chilly condensation wet the back of my jeans, easing my legs a little. The light was milky as it often is inside the hoop house in late fall. The temperature was a good ten degrees warmer than outside, in the real world. I sat down cross-legged at the edge of the radishes, where for some reason the grass is always long and lush.

"Where *are* you, Trey?" I whispered, then I went quiet, listening.

The wind was rising and it sucked at the plastic. A grasshopper jettisoned himself from the arugula. It reminded me of Zero, the way it defied gravity with such ease. How could something so dynamic just suddenly go . . . still?

I lay back with my hands under my head. The thick, clear plastic had weathered now and was slightly yellowed. Through it I watched the invisible wind have its way with the limbs of the big cottonwood tree, making the wood groan, making the longest branches thrash and tangle like moody, irritable skeleton arms. Small twigs kept falling against the top of the hoop house in a rhythmic way, like a cadence, like . . .

Hey down there, Tucker Graysten, you innocent wonder, you!

I scrambled to my feet. Trey? I shot out of the hoop house and turned to scope the yard, but all I saw was evidence of the wind at work—leaves skittering, limbs groaning, little sticks falling on the hoop house like drumbeats.

At the edge of sleep I'd dreamed that I'd heard Trey call me, that's all it was. But something gray and sickening began gnawing its way into my mind. It had to do with Trey's tone of voice. He'd called me an innocent wonder three or four times a week for the last couple of months.

So why had he sounded so sarcastic when I'd dreamed of him saying it just now?

I slapped leaf clutter off me and went back toward the house, forgetting the vegetables a second time. I was partway through the kitchen door when I noticed Janet at the counter, barefoot in jeans and a T-shirt.

Her hair was down at her shoulders, but it had a dent halfway up from her work ponytail. She had the big plastic box she uses for tools open on the counter and was throwing stuff out and scolding it. "Why can't I *ever* find *anything* in you?"

I took a step backward, but then I noticed something that stopped me from sneaking the rest of the way back outside. My mother's picture, on the kitchen table.

Janet whirled around. "Tucker, where'd *you* come from?" She pushed her hair from her eyes with her wrist and looked at me looking at the picture. "Now don't go giving me a hard time, Tucker, because I've had about enough of a hard time today, as I'm sure you have as well. I just got back from work and I'm in charge of the funeral dinner the restaurant is providing for the families tomorrow, so I've gotta be making calls to get contributions of pies and things for that. And so before I started my calls, I had five minutes to spare and I decided to re-hang your mother. I mean, she's been down at your eight-year-old level for far too long, and I left her there because when you're sitting and watching TV and so forth you are at the right level to glance over and see her. But right now, with all that's happened, you need to be able to walk into the living room and find her looking at you eye-to-eye again."

She sighed and dropped into a chair at the table. "I don't know why I think anything'll be a five-minute job when everything in this house is just held together with spit and bubble gum." She put her hands on her forehead and pushed back her hair as she looked down at the picture. "I'm so sorry, Cynthia Anne," she said quietly.

Her face had that pink and blotchy look of someone who's been crying off and on for a long time. It hit me then that everyone who came into the restaurant today or yesterday had probably asked her about the bonfire and the whole rest of the thing.

"Tucker?" She straightened her shoulders and looked up at me. "Since the families are coming to the restaurant straight from the service I have to miss the funerals to supervise the cooking and organizing. But honey, I talked to your principal and he says some kids from your class will be sitting together. One of them will meet you at the door so you won't even have to walk in alone."

I focused on the red pain and walked across to the sink, then edged sideways a step and peered into her box of tangled tools. "What'd you want out of here?" I stirred it.

"Oh, glue," she said in a dull, hopeless voice. "But don't think it'll be so easy. I've got ten kinds of glue in there. Mucilage, monkey glue, rubber cement, Elmer's Wood Glue, Elmer's School Glue, at least three bottles of that from different times I bought it for you in Cub Scouts, though it's probably dried up. I've got superglue and amazing superglue and tacky glue. And besides that I'm gonna need the right kind of little vise grips to hold this until it sets, and I've got six or seven kinds of those."

I closed my eyes while my back was still to her and gritted my teeth to contain the pain in my legs enough to turn around and walk casually out of the kitchen without her commenting on it.

"Tucker, what do you think is so easy about taking care of you and Bud?" she suddenly said sharply. "One so pigheaded and the other so silent?"

This came out of nowhere. I stirred the tools around again to look busy. The loud clock there on the wall clicked off every second.

"Oh, just go back out and get me some broccoli," she finally said. "And don't worry, I'll go work on my call list for the dinner in the other room so you won't have to try not to walk like you're walking." She stomped out.

I got the broccoli and some radishes and chard, rinsed them in the kitchen, then found some glue in Janet's box, fixed the picture frame, and clamped it. I went upstairs then to work on algebra until dinner, but I ended up pulling my desk chair over to the window instead so I could just slump in it and stare at Trey's rock. *Hey down there, Tucker Graysten, you innocent wonder, you . . .* I grimaced. Why had Trey sounded so . . . unfriendly? Why had I dreamed him like that unless wherever he was, he . . . was?

We ate dinner, then I hurried back to my room and took Trey's green Bic from my pocket. It was dark by then, but I didn't turn on the light. I could see the whiteness of the outside window ledge and the scrap of shadow on it that was the pebble.

I sat in the chair and held the Bic out in front of me, close to the window.

"Trey, I'm only going to do this once," I whispered. "If you're mad at me or . . . or *blame* me or something, your lighter will light on the fourth click." My hand was shaking, so I gripped my wrist with my other hand—click, click, click, click, click, click, *fwoom!* Seven times.

"Okay, Trey, I'm only going to do *this* once. Your lighter will light on the sixth click if you are *not* mad at me." I opened the lighter—click, click, click, *fwoom!*

I saw a flicker of movement in the window glass. My blood went icy, but when I turned to look closely, I saw it was just Bud's reflection. He'd come upstairs and was standing planted in the hallway between our rooms, looking in at me.

I turned my head. "G'night, Bud," I murmured, trying to steady my heartbeat.

"Yeah." He raised an arm and dropped it. "Listen, there'll always be questions in your mind, I remember that from Korea, how it tears your gut not to know this and that. You wanta ask them, but you don't have a way. Anyhow, why should the dead know so much about it, huh? If my Mary knew answers, she woulda told me by now why she left ahead of me." He raised an arm again and this time turned and went into his room.

I closed my door, then went back and slumped in the chair again, staring out.

Hey down there, you innocent wonder, you . . . The cold and sarcastic tone of his voice, how his eyes had to be hooded and hard. Trey was accusing me of something.

Not many people came to school the next morning. They took the early out we'd been given for permission to skip all day, which I'd thought about doing myself. But you have to do *something* even on the morning they're digging graves for your three best friends. Clevesdale High School, with its bright, humming fluorescent lights and shiny silver-flecked blue floor tiles and general air of safety and boredom, would be so much better than my room, where that rock of Trey's still balanced on my windowsill, teetering mysteriously several times a night with or without there being wind.

And so I spent my first-period study hall in the library, flipping through sports magazines and not really seeing what I was looking at. Then I accidentally picked up an *American Life* and it slipped through my fingers to the floor, falling open to a picture of the airliner that crashed in that Ohio field last month. There was the doomed plane just before the crash, shiny against an innocent blue sky, tilted in a weird way as though it was the pencil in the hand of some crazy god. You could even make out a tiny row of windows running zipper-like right above its burning wing. If I had Bud's magnifying glass, the one he kept beside the TV book, I could even possibly make out the faces of some of the passengers. Then I might be able to figure out what they were thinking, those people in that shiny tube, looking out those thick round windows at a future that was no future at all.

My hands began to shake as I shoved that magazine into my backpack, then grabbed a second newsmagazine, a *Time*, where I found a full-page black-and-white photo of an AIDS victim hooked to machines. The man in that narrow bed was very young and as thin as Zero, and he looked straight out of the picture with hollow, accusing eyes. What did he know that no one knew who wasn't in his shoes?

Next, in a *Newsweek*, I found a picture of a bridge collapse that sent six cars plunging like stones to the bottom of a river. Four of the cars were visible in the picture, three caught in the act of sinking and one teetering on the tongue-like edge of a jagged splinter of asphalt. A blurry face stared from the backseat window of that teetering car.

The fourth picture was of a soldier in some recent war. He was defying the law of gravity, helped along by some sort of explosion behind him that, the caption said, took his life. But in the picture he was very much alive, flying like everyone dreamed of doing, like Zero thought he could do if he leaped from that chat pile, and thinking . . . what?

A *National Geographic* I grabbed had a double-page spread of a cage of monkeys on their way to receive lethal injections because they had some kind of weird tropical virus. The thing about that picture was the way one of the monkeys was sucking on a piece of banana with his eyes slightly closed. Unlike the guy trapped by tubes to his narrow bed or the people in those teetering or sinking cars, or probably even the flying soldier, that monkey had no inkling of what was about to happen to him.

That monkey looked as simply and perfectly happy as Trey always looked. *Don't you dare puke in my car, Graysten!* Trey, cheerful even as he peeled away from me, sailing down that dark bluff road for the very last time. Trey, grinning, easy with life, with his last two minutes of it, of life.

I didn't worry about whether Mr. Mayes, the librarian, noticed me stuffing my backpack with those magazines. That actually wasn't likely, since he's always on the Internet. But I didn't even worry about whether I was overstaying study hall. I had to follow this where it led, had to get that magnifying glass of Bud's to see these amazing pictures better so I could feel my way into that place where . . .

"Tucker?"

My heart took a lurch and I reluctantly raised my eyes to see

Ms. Jazzmeyer's orange and black fingernails resting on my left shoulder like some bizarre tropical spider.

"Come with *me*, Tucker, okay?"

It wasn't really a question, since I had no choice. She let me go and turned to lead the way to her office, and I slipped that fifth magazine into my pack, wiped my sweaty hands on my jeans, and followed her.

She sat down behind her desk and gestured for me to drop into one of her two huge turquoise chairs. "I'm afraid the grief counselors from Tulsa were a bit delayed, Tucker," she explained in a sorrowful voice. "No worries, they'll be here tomorrow. Still, we shouldn't wait that long to get *you* started working on your feelings."

I swallowed and tried to resist touching my lips with my fingers to see if I was managing to work my face into an acceptable expression. "I can wait, no problem."

She crossed her arms and narrowed her eyes.

"Tuck, your teachers and classmates are terribly worried about you. You look like you haven't eaten or slept since it happened, but you won't confide in *any*one. A couple of young women have reported to me that you even hung up on their calls of concern. You *need* to talk about this, Tuck. Now nothing you say will shock me, and I promise our conversation won't go beyond this office. Just open up and tell me how you *feel.*"

It took me a while to come up with something. "I feel . . . surprised?"

She leaned forward, looking interested, which was the *last* thing I wanted. I desperately needed out of that suffocating turquoise chair, a chair that belonged in someone's living room, not in a high school office. But I was trapped by its bloated plastic arms in this room of ferny plants and Ms. Jazzmeyer's extensive glass bear collection. Also, it looked like the walls were slowly coming together to crush me.

I should have been with them! Should I start howling that I'd let my three best friends go on without me and that I'd had no business staying behind? I might have done something, stopped them somehow, warned Trey to slow for that curve, jumped up and leaned far over the white leather back of the driver's seat in time to give the wheel a hard yank left? I'd always been their guard, their lookout. That's what a lookout did, he looked out for his people! Did she want me to start *screeching* all that like a person being turned inside out? I was supposed to be with them, I should have been with them, I was always with them, did she want me to start crying real tears about that and the related fact that I was now and would always be soul-tattooed, not to mention haunted by a small rock I didn't dare brush off the outside sill of my bedroom window? Why didn't I just get on the office intercom and explain all that so the whole school could hear it at once and whip out their phones to text me their concern?

And now this new thing, this dream thing, Trey unfriendly to me like I'd never once seen him, Trey's sarcastic voice squeezing in like a rat to gnaw at my aching brain. *Tucker Graysten, you innocent wonder, you* . . . Was Trey's postmortem sarcasm what she and her interested gallery of little glass bears wanted me to chat about?

"Ms. Jazzmeyer?" I whispered. "Let's say you're in an airliner falling from the sky. For those last few seconds, would you think of yourself as still alive, as a thinking person with a head full of plans, or if not, what *would* be in your head?"

She let me go soon after that. When I got to my locker, I dug out my protractor from the clutter at the bottom. I dropped my backpack onto the floor, took out the first magazine, and flipped it open to that jetliner. I measured the angle of its descent at fifty-two degrees, then I packed up and went home to change shirts for the funeral. Funerals.

VII

I HAD BEEN INSIDE McElderry's Funeral Home only once before, when my mom died. I couldn't see anything then, the heads all around me were too tall. Somebody gave me my first ever Tootsie Roll Pop, either from sympathy or to keep me quiet.

And now here I was climbing the very same stone steps her casket had been carried down eleven years ago. The very same steps.

"Oh, Tucker, good, there you are!" Aimee was just inside the big oak doorway, standing there in the dimness holding a white rose in each black-gloved hand. She held one of the roses out to me. "Here, take this. We saved you a seat. We're right near the front, right behind the section reserved for the families."

I took the rose and she put her arm through mine and maneuvered us over the thick lobby carpeting and into the large room with all the church-like pews and the dozens of overpoweringly ugly flower arrangements.

She walked us slowly, showing me off like I was a catch, like I was Josh Hinstrom, for instance, the basketball team captain who'd been junior high homecoming king when Aimee was junior high homecoming queen back when we were all in eighth grade. I'm not Josh Hinstrom, not anyone she'd normally walk with, so I knew she was appointing me captain of this particular event, sole survivor, chief witness of the carnage, interesting for today, just like Zero had been interesting to her for a week or so until she figured out that he wasn't going to be tamed into anyone normal enough for her.

People turned to watch us go by, and Aimee touched a white cloth handkerchief to her eyes, reaching beneath the black veil attached to the front of her vintage hat.

I began to notice that there was no smell whatsoever in the room. The place smelled more like nothing than anyplace I'd ever been. The hundreds of flowers smelled especially like nothing, as if their smells had been drawn out of them with a long syringe.

For a panicked few seconds, I couldn't breathe. I made a gasping sound before I realized I was confusing lack of smell with lack of air. Aimee squeezed my arm hard as she shot me a don't-you-dare-embarrass-me look from behind that black veil of hers.

The organ kept playing long, sad chords that didn't seem to go anywhere. I strained to hear some sort of resolution, or even some sort of beauty, but it never came.

Steve's last music should have been Memphis blues, not this. Anything but this.

We reached the pew near the front where Aimee had organized the cheerleaders and class officers and people like that. She sat us down and I saw that everyone had a white rose at the ready, twirling it or letting it rest on the padding of the pew. Jawbones clenching and unclenching above stiff-collared dress shirts. Red, red lipstick and nail polish on the girls, and that hat of Aimee's with a coolness factor right off the charts.

We were the stars of a heartbreaking movie about fast cars and sudden death. The good-looking friends, the tragic survivors. Except that these people, this row of the class royalty, hadn't *been* Zero's friends, or Trey's, or Steve's. Trey and Steve and Zero were their own friends, we four were, the three of them and me. They were *my* friends. Mine.

I glared, hard, at each of the three shining boxes strategically placed right up front among the worst of those massive clots of flowers. *Do you see me, guys, alone here?*

The organ gained some volume and the families were paraded to the front, held up by ushers. They looked doped up and out of it, especially Steve's mother. She looked like she was just learning how to walk. Jasper Nordike was pretty much holding her up. His face looked so weird that for a second I thought he was doing something strange with his wife's makeup to be in solidarity with Steve's trip down the bluff. Then I got a grip and figured out Jasper Nordike had an extreme cowboy tan, his forehead ghostly white from his Stetson, everything beneath it rawhide dark. Two people with Steve's mother and Jasper Nordike but not looking at them must have been Steve's dad and stepmother.

Zero's grandfather had the hot, roving eyes of a lunatic, and Trey's kid sister, Emilie, spotted me and waved a tiny sad wave. I automatically winked and gave her the thumbs-up sign, the sign

I gave her about a million times when Trey put me in charge of teaching her how to ride her bike a couple of years ago. Stupid! That had been a stupid, stupid gesture that made me sick.

So I wouldn't do anything that stupid again, I slouched down, crossed my arms, and braced my neck over the hard curve at the top of the pew. I focused my eyes almost straight upward and concentrated on the border that ran just beneath the high ceiling of the room. Somebody had painted a long, skinny picture up there of old marble buildings surrounded by deep woods. Lots of sleepy-looking people in white robes lolled around the woods and sailed golden boats along a blue river that ran between the trees.

If that picture was supposed to be heaven, it looked way too slow for Trey and Steve, let alone Zero. I knew it wasn't exactly supposed to be heaven, though. It was just some imaginary place meant to lull you into thinking things would always stay the kind of bland that must pass for beautiful if you were as old as you were supposed to be to die. Beautiful like the odorless flowers and the going-nowhere organ chords and the cloud-thick pink carpet. I began peeling strips of green from the stem of my rose.

The organ droned on. Time went by. People walked to the podium and read things. A trio of girls from the senior class sang a sad song. Aimee finally dug into my ribs with her elbow, indicating it was nearly time for our big moment here on royalty row, for us to lead the exit from this place by filing past the grief-stricken families and then the three caskets, leaving our perfect white roses in heartbreaking disarray on their closed lids.

I looked down and saw that my hands were suddenly shaking quite badly. My heart had somehow morphed into a flopping fish in the oxygenless river that ran along the border beneath the ceiling. I was drowning in that fake water. I broke out in a sweat that soaked my shirt, and my lips went numb. I couldn't remember how buttons worked, so I grabbed my collar and ripped it open with a jerk of my fist.

And then I shot to my feet, panting, swaying a little in that ocean of seated people.

Aimee clutched at my sleeve, trying to pull me down. I saw an usher hurrying toward me. A few of the family members turned to see what was going on behind them.

When Zero's mother saw me standing there alone, she stood as well. In fact, she eased quickly past some of the knees between her and me and then leaned over the back of her pew to grasp my wrist. We locked eyes and I saw that hers were completely blank, as though all the crazy fun inside her, all the silliness and laughter, had been carved out and thrown away.

One rainy week near the end of last May, I spent hours each afternoon with Zero and his mother, watching movies at the crazy, cluttered trailer where the two of them lived. I was there because Zero had a free trial week of the movie channel, and with all the rain neither of us could work outside at our lawn-mowing jobs or even think about organizing a barbecue. All the dishes were usually dirty, so we used paper cones made from the

Sunday comics to hold the cheese popcorn Zero's mother was always making for us.

Once, when the movie was bad, silly-bad, a real howler, Zero and I started throwing popcorn at each other. From where she'd sprawled on the couch, Zero's mother jabbed her bare toes into our sides, tickling us like we were little kids. Then Zero and I rolled around wrestling on the littered carpet while his mother threw *her* popcorn at us and laughed herself into a coughing fit.

Now she whispered my name in that hushed place. "Tucker?"

I looked at her, waiting.

You saw him, didn't you? she asked me with her hollowed-out eyes.

"Yes, I saw him," I whispered back to her.

And then she looked slowly down the rest of that aisle of white-rose-bearing junior class royalty. She focused on them one by one, and they all dropped their eyes quickly so that not one of them had to meet her bruised, withering gaze.

When she'd finished that, she gave a hard smile and looked at me again.

"They need to see too," she breathed so quietly no one else could have heard.

She beckoned to the usher that loomed nearby, and he scuttled to her side and leaned one ear close. She gave him whispered instructions, and you could tell from his expression that he didn't like what he was hearing. He whispered something back, but she glared a response so firm that he gave a sigh and nodded, then grimly signaled for the other three ushers to join him up front.

Together, they unlatched the lid of Zero's casket and propped it wide open.

Aimee shrank back, but I suddenly felt true hot anger making me brave and foolhardy. I took her arm and pulled her to her feet, almost yanked her, and together we walked past the two closed caskets and then stopped before the single open one.

She glanced at Zero, then she jerked her arm from me and hurried on down the aisle that led outside. All the kids that came behind us did pretty much the same, dropped their roses, trampled them into the carpet as they gave Zero a quick look, then made toward the exit with wide eyes, gulping or even retching. A couple of the varsity football players loped down the exit aisle with their hands over their mouths.

I stayed at the casket until everyone on royalty row had left, then I looked at Zero's mother. She stood again and began unwinding a long and beautiful cloth she had around her own neck. It was this batik stuff she makes, a real art form, Janet says. She held the blue scarf out to me and I got it and took it back to Zero's casket.

It wasn't that his head was still missing clear to his eyebrows, like it had been at the beach. No, the funeral people had molded him a replacement skull with some sort of clay. But it was so obviously fake that it was really *worse* than no skull at all. For one thing, it was slightly the wrong color, too gray for his skin. And all his beautiful dreads were gone; what hadn't been taken by the rough stone of the bluff had now been shaved.

I leaned down and wrapped the batik around and around his head, giving him the protection of all those Haitian animals his mother had designed—manatees, fish, turtles.

I glanced at her again over my shoulder, and when she nodded, I closed the casket forever on Zero's interesting, intelligent face. Then I walked outside, into the clear air.

Aimee was waiting. She slapped my face.

"What's the *matter* with you, Tucker? Don't you have any respect at *all*? Doesn't his own *mother*? You should . . . you should be ashamed of yourselves!"

I looked down at the grass. I wanted to drop to my knees and smell it, just to smell something with a smell. I wanted to disappear into it like rain.

Instead, I turned away from Aimee, slung my jacket over my shoulder, jerked my tie the rest of the way off, and trudged home.

Bud was on the porch swing when I got there. Ringo was sleeping with his head on Bud's left foot, and the weird dog was standing nearby with its three tongues lolling. One of its feet was on Bud's shoe. It looked sort of . . . blurry. I broke out in a cold sweat, then immediately recovered. What I saw was impossible, sure, but I had just been innoculated to impossibility and for a while I was going to be immune to it. Nothing could have been quite as impossible as the nightmare of a funeral, not even a giant of a three-headed spiral-eyed dog. So bring it on.

That weird dog looked sort of blurry. Like it was made of light or something?

"Bud? That's . . . the dog," I told him in a hoarse whisper.

Bud and the dog both looked at me. Bud had his hands on his knees, and he was sitting in his usual straight-backed way. The dog had the hazy look things have when you come out of the swimming pool with water and chlorine in your eyes.

"Whaddaya talking about?" Bud growled. "You don't look so hot, by the way. Must've been bad, that funeral, those boys so young?"

"Pretty bad, all right," I told him listlessly. My legs hadn't been a factor during the funeral, but now they suddenly throbbed. Did things hurt worse when infection set in?

"You need a diversion," Bud said, "something different to put your mind on. I got just the thing. Listen, I called the fools at the driver's license office today, the ones what gave me the eye test last week? I figured out it was rigged, so I called and told them so. Threatened to have the authorities after 'em for elder abuse and eye discrimination. You can bet that scared 'em plenty. They're giving me the test again, tomorrow. You're taking me, see?"

He pulled a key fob from his shirt pocket and tossed it to me. I caught it and looked down at it. These two keys weren't to the Taurus. They were different, longer, older-looking. They had four capital letters stamped into their greenish copper—*OLDS*.

"So . . . that car in the garage is . . . is yours, Bud?"

That old green Oldsmobile had just been collecting garage

grit out there for years. I'd assumed it belonged to my dad, that it was one of the many things he left behind when he walked away. No one drove it. No one talked about it. It just sat like some bloated green insect, using space Janet could have used to park the Taurus instead.

Bud gave a snort. "Think Janet would have a muscle car like that?"

"Guess not," I murmured.

"It's a shame I don't have my old Ford truck. They'd see something if I was at the wheel of that big old Ford, I'll tell you that. This Olds has plenty of style, though. They made 'em pretty in the seventies. Lotsa power in a V-8 engine."

The dog had been fading and now was gone. I climbed the stairs, stepping wide around where it had been. "Later, Bud," I said, pocketing the fob.

"Yeah, we go tomorrow!" he called after me. "Don't forget! No need to tell Janet."

I couldn't think about any of this. It was all I could do to block the pain of my legs enough to slowly climb the stairs to my room, leaning hard on the banister. I dropped my jacket and tie on the floor and fell face forward across my bed, where I lay the rest of the afternoon listening to the tiny chattering of Trey's rock there on the windowsill. I remember it starting to get dark. Then I guess I fell asleep.

I woke up the next morning still in my funeral clothes, though my shoes were off and a blanket had been thrown over me. I felt a small pain where Bud's keys were grinding into my leg near my right hip bone. I rolled onto my back and pulled out that key fob.

I held it up and stared at it. Bud was expecting me to drive him to the license office this afternoon, but I just *couldn't* any more than I could sprout wings and fly. I couldn't drive anyone anywhere ever again, that was just a fact of life.

I dug a wadded candy bar wrapper from under my bed and wrote a single word on it, then added another word. *Can't. Sorry.*

I went quietly down the stairs with my boots tucked under my arm, feeling every inch like the coward I was. I dropped Bud's key fob and my two-word note on the table by his La-Z-Boy as I left, trying not to think how he would feel when he saw them.

The damp wind pushed my hair across my face as I slunk along. My hair had that nothing smell of the funeral home. The rest of me smelled like sweaty, slept-in clothes and jeans that were going rank with dry and not-so-dry blood from the backs of my legs.

I got to the school at least an hour early, maybe two hours, but the night custodians were there and one of the side doors was propped open with a cleaning bucket. I slipped inside and wandered around.

Without people the school had a metallic, spaceship feel. It also hummed, and I noticed there was a slight, mysterious vibration coming up from under the floors. It could have been the heating system, but then again, it could have been anything.

I eventually found myself standing in front of Zero and

Steve's side-by-side lockers. They both had shiny new combination locks on them that hadn't been there before. Steve's old lock had been busted, and Zero had recently been using his to chain his skateboard to the school bike rack. What were these new locks supposed to be for?

Possibly to protect their stuff till somebody could take it home. But more likely the police were planning on dragging Clyde the drug dog out here in hopes of sniffing out something illegal that had caused the wreck to happen. It seemed like the police would assume that druggies with stuff hidden inside their lockers would be careful to have locks, but what did I know about it? Nothing. I knew nothing about that or much of anything else.

Too much thinking was making my head hurt, so I walked on to Trey's locker, which is next to my own. It also had a new combination lock on it. I couldn't even remember Trey's last lock since for so long he'd preferred the risk of having stuff stolen to the work of remembering his combination. I sat on the floor with my back against the cold green metal and imagined how Trey's brown leather jacket was probably still under the multiple layers of mess in the bottom of this locker, the arms shaped like Trey's arms from the great age of the thing and its general grungy stiffness.

Hey down there, Tucker Graysten, you innocent wonder, you . . .

I felt sick each time I remembered the way Trey had sounded when he'd dropped that quick sentence into my hoop house dream, his sarcastic tone of voice. I bumped my head back hard against his locker, then again, this time harder.

And then I heard the squeak of distant tennis shoes on floor tile and turned my head to *see* Trey rounding the corner by the principal's office and coming in my direction. I wasn't even all that surprised. He was coming to get me, picking me up so we could go together to wherever it was he *had* to go. I'd be going along for the ride, I got that. I deserved to be where they were, so I stood, resisting the urge to run as he came closer and closer through the glaring path the fluorescent lights cut down the center of the windowless, shadow-shrouded gloom of the locker hall. Calm down, *breathe!*

"Trey, I'd give my life in a second, I *would,* if I could just try again to . . ."

Trey's brother shrugged off his backpack and called, "Try again to what, dude?" He laughed a sharp laugh. "Hey, Tucker, get ahold of yourself!"

He shoved his long red hair behind his ears and jogged toward me the last twenty or so feet. "I'm *Aidan,* dude! See? Not Trey. Aidan!"

I nodded and then couldn't remember how to stop nodding.

Aidan grabbed me by the shoulders and pushed me back against Trey's locker, pinning me there until I could get myself together enough for my legs to hold me.

"I'm fine," I whispered, staring at the floor.

"Yeah, *that's* clear." Aidan snickered and let me go. "That was clear at the funeral yesterday and it's clear by how you're acting right now. In my opinion you're pretty messed up, dude. Maybe you need more sleep or a girlfriend or something."

He said all this lightly, in the same slightly condescending way he'd always talked to Trey's friends, then he motioned with a waggle of his fingers for me to step aside so he could explore Trey's new lock. "Who put this thing on here, anyhow?"

I rubbed my neck. "I'm thinking maybe the police."

Aidan let go of the lock and stood up from his crouch, frowning. "Listen, where's my ID? I figure it might be in this locker of Trey's, huh? I can't get into the library or a bunch of other places on campus without it."

I murmured, "I think Trey . . . had it with him. Yeah, I know he did."

"Had it with him?" It took Aidan a few seconds to figure that out, then he gave a nod, followed by a grimace. "It's gonna suck, trying to get another one. They got all kinds of security stuff you have to go through."

I stared at him and didn't say anything. He looked so much like Trey it was incredible. But there was also something the opposite of Trey about Aidan.

It was in the eyes, maybe. Aidan's eyes had not met mine this whole time. Even when he'd had me backed against the locker his eyes had been roaming around, scoping things out.

"Did you . . ." I stopped and swallowed. "Aidan, did you give Trey your ID?"

Aidan was looking up and down the hallway. "This place is exactly the same as three years ago." He snorted and shook his head. "When? Give him my ID when, last weekend? Wow, even those same old posters outside the music room. I kinda liked the one with a dagger through a phone. Turn your phone off in the theater performances, get it?"

It *was* in the eyes. Trey's eyes settled on you and stayed there. Aidan's were always sliding across things and never seemed to stick anywhere. Never penetrated anything.

"Not *just* last weekend," I pushed out. "I know he used it nearly every weekend that you didn't have to have it yourself, but I just wondered, did you always *give* it to him, or was he sneaking it out of your wallet without your permission?"

Aidan looked insulted. "Hey, you think I'm so stupid he could sneak it out of my wallet? Sure I gave it to him when I didn't need it. Why not?"

We were both startled by the clatter of the first bell, followed immediately by the usual raucous morning stampede of the junior horde on its way to our locker hallway.

Aidan grabbed me in a headlock, then released me and hustled away. "You get your act together before you hurt yourself!" he called back over his shoulder.

I stood swaying, dizzy. Trey had talked about his little sister, but hardly ever about Aidan. Last year, Aidan stole Trey's prized comic book collection and sold it back to him for a nickel a copy, tearing up a few of Trey's favorite copies first to show him what would happen if he didn't pay up.

"Why would he *do* that?" Steve had exploded in outrage. Aidan's selfishness had completely offended his hard-wired

Southern sense of honor. "He took a thing that you really cared about, and he couldn't even have made much ransom money from it!"

Trey just shrugged and said, "He's Aidan. That's how he rolls."

Now, I understood what Trey had meant by that. And for a second or two there in the hall, I even longed to be *like* Aidan. If he ever got soul tattoos they evidently washed off right away, like the cheap temporary tats they sometimes put on your wrist when you pay admission to a game.

VIII

I GOT MY STUFF from my own locker then and followed my throbbing legs to my classes. Or maybe I just kept wandering around the school like before. Or maybe I chatted with the aliens in the basement, the crew of the secret spaceship the school actually was. Maybe I spent the day in the library. Or in the gym, running laps. No, not that, not with my legs burning up a storm like they were.

I can't honestly remember much about that day except that I had a vague impression of people avoiding me. This would be partly because of what happened at the funeral and mostly because of Aimee's subsequent interpretation of those events, which was probably everybody's interpretation by now.

Also maybe my hygiene, my unwashed hair, those rank jeans. Anyhow, it's all hazy, except for last period, which was Mrs. Beetlebaum's class, Ancient History.

Mrs. Beetlebaum's room is a world unto itself. It smells like very old papery dust. There are probably more books in her history room than in the school library, floor-to-ceiling books, all of them belonging to Mrs. Beetlebaum herself.

Mrs. Beetlebaum is probably nearly as old as Bud, much older than the other teachers. She wears black old-lady shoes and she stands in front of her classes each day with her heels together and her toes pointed out. She always folds her blue-veined hands on her stomach when she gets ready to tell a story, and telling stories from the ancient past is a thing she does a lot. She would be easy to mock, but nobody much does. The stories are exciting and she tells them very well.

We were studying ancient Greece. She'd been telling us stories from the Trojan War complete with lots of gory details, whose lifeless bodies were drug by horses around the Trojan city walls, what wild predictions this out-of-control girl named Cassandra kept making, that kind of thing.

But that day, Mrs. Beetlebaum took her place at the front of the room wearing the black shawl she usually has hanging over the back of her desk chair. She had released her long gray hair from its usual tight bun at the nape of her neck, a thing we'd never seen her do before. And everybody instantly quieted down as she slowly raised the shawl from her shoulders, shook back her hair, then covered it completely with that shawl, an ancient sign of mourning we'd studied in this very class.

She was obviously about to begin some sad story or poem in tribute to Trey and Steve and Zero. A couple of girls sniffled ostentatiously, probably wishing *they'd* thought of something as dramatic as that when the funeral-look plans were being made.

And then Mrs. Beetlebaum began reading us this long Greek poem about death and stuff. In it, this supernatural guy, some sort of god or something, was steering a boatload of dead guys across the river Acheron to the realm of Hades, god of the underworld. That was this guy's job, to ferry people from the land of the living to the land of the dead. This particular trip, the one in the poem, this ferryman guy was taking these young dead war heroes to the best of places, kind of the country club of the underworld, a place called the Elysian fields, where they'd always be young and cool and strong, et cetera.

I could have listened to that poem forever, it was that soothing. Not because Steve and Zero and Trey were heroes. But because it was so natural to think of them in a boat like that. The four of us used to borrow Zero's uncle's speedboat sometimes or rent Jet Skis for the afternoon to use on the lake. The poem said the boat was black, which seemed like a huge coincidence since Zero's uncle's boat had also been black.

When she'd finished reading, Mrs. Beetlebaum propped the open book against the bulletin board and took a strange coin from the pocket of her skirt.

"An obolus," she told us, displaying it between her thumb and index finger. "A coin placed in the mouth of the newly dead. It was the price of passage from the land of the living to the land of the dead, payment for the ferryman across the river Acheron."

I couldn't get that boat out of my mind. The book she'd been reading from was illustrated, and by leaning far forward I could make out some details of the pictures. The ferryman from the poem was black-bearded and very ugly, but his boat was pretty cool and looked in some additional ways like Zero's uncle's speedboat. Both were simple but sleek and shiny. You could see a slight resemblance to Steve in the hero in the far back of the boat, something about the moony longing in his eyes, like he felt homesick. You could also see a little of the shore where the boat would soon dock, and . . .

My blood suddenly felt all sharp and icy in my veins.

When the bell rang, everybody stampeded, but I stayed where I was until Mrs. Beetlebaum and I were alone in the room. She watched me, slowly shaking her head.

"You look absolutely dreadful," she told me solemnly. "But then I suppose you should. Those three boys were your great friends, am I right?"

I pushed myself up from my desk and walked stiffly to her book. "Mrs. Beetlebaum? Is . . . : is that a dog in the picture there?"

She turned to the bulletin board. "Cerberus," she told me, picking up the book and holding it open between us. "Guardian of Hades, charged with letting no spirit escape the underworld."

I stared at that large black dog. "But it . . . has three heads."

"Yes, Cerberus is usually depicted with three heads." She shut the book and put it down on her desk, then opened a drawer and took out a small framed photograph. She sighed, then handed it to me. "My husband, taken the summer before he died."

The picture was old, black and white. The man in it was pretty young, probably in his thirties or early forties. About Janet's age,

I would guess. He was in his swimming trunks, standing on a sandy beach, the kind they have in Florida or California, with palm trees in the background. Something about the way he was grinning made me think Mrs. Beetlebaum as her much younger self must have taken the picture.

I handed it back to her. Since I had no idea what to say, I said nothing.

"It was a mere five weeks from the diagnosis of cancer to his death. I wanted to follow him. I thought if I was stalwart enough to follow him, I could take his hand and bring him back up to the light with me. Others, overwhelmed by death's finality, have tried in one way or another to do the same thing. There are stories of Greek heroes who braved the underworld, seeking a lost father or wife or friend. But not a single one of them, not Aeneas or Orpheus or even Odysseus, was able to clutch a hand long enough to lead a loved one back to the world of the living. It's just a . . . a dream, really."

She put the photo back into the drawer, then she lifted my hand and put the strange coin she'd showed the class onto my palm. She closed my fingers over it.

"Take it. Keep it in your pocket." She looked me in the eye with the most amazing sorrow on her face. "Tucker, do you understand me? I have stood where you stand now. I won't try to explain, not right now, but there may soon come a time when you'll want with all your heart to give it up. The coin, that is. But don't. Remember what I'm telling you right here, right now, and . . . *don't.*"

Take it. Don't give it up. Take, give, give, take.

My ears were ringing. I concentrated on the red pain in my legs.

"Okay, thanks, Mrs. Beetlebaum." I let my legs move me toward the door.

"Tucker, that coin is still in your hand! Put it in your pocket and *keep* it there!"

"Right. Sorry." I put the coin into my pocket, where I felt it bump against Trey's cheap green lighter. I moved it to my back pocket, gave it a space of its own.

I turned once more to Mrs. Beetlebaum and she gave me a grim nod.

My legs led me down the hall. When I got to Trey's locker, I sagged forward and pushed my forehead hard against the three sharp air vents at the top. I closed my eyes.

Take, give. I took a beer, took another beer, Zero gave me a third, but I was the one to take it. *Yeah, man, take the wheel so I can do this thing . . . take, take, take the wheel. . . .*

I pushed back, then bounced my forehead once, hard, against Trey's vents, so hard that bright pain bloomed across my bones up there and I felt something begin a slow slide down both sides of my nose. I put my hand to my face and my fingers came away smeared red. I wiped my forehead and found a bigger smear of red on my palm.

I stood there with my bloody hand held out like an artist's tool, staring at the green slate of the locker. What could I say, what message to Trey? *Later, man,* I finally wrote. Most of the letters were already dripping out of recognition as I followed my legs out of the building, along the sidewalk, et cetera, et cetera, until I reached our neighborhood.

Our house looked strange when I got close. At first I couldn't figure out why, and then I realized that the garage door was open for the first time I could remember. It made a dark square, like a missing tooth, and Bud's old car was gone from inside it.

I quit walking and stood there squinting, trying to focus, trying to figure out what that empty garage meant. A feeling of dread had started in my stomach and was working its way through me, but still, I didn't understand what was going on, why the car was gone.

"Tucker! Over here, Tuck! We need to talk to you!"

I wheeled and saw Mrs. Brandywine giving me wide-armed waves from across the street and down the block a few houses. Mr. Brandywine was with her, squatting to look closely at something on the ground in their yard.

When I reached them, Mrs. Brandywine put her hands to her face and whispered, "Oh, Tuck, have you been in a fight at school? Or an accident? Oh, you poor thing!"

My face, the blood. "It's nothing. Just fell in some gravel at track today." I didn't meet her eyes, just kept my own eyes on the muddy furrow Mr. Brandywine was inspecting. A strip of orange flowers had been pulverized by a gigantic tire. Bright bits of flower decorated the deep and muddy tire track like rhinestones.

"Tucker, I was gardening and your grandfather, well, he drove over some of our nasturtiums," Mrs. Brandywine explained. "Is he supposed to be, well . . . driving?"

There was a black mark on their curb near the driveway and another mark on the curb maybe twenty feet along where Bud had finally bounced the big Olds out of their yard and back to the street.

"At the corner he turned right onto Maple," Mr. Brandywine said, still glaring at the mess that had been their flowers. He stood up and shook his head, muttering, "There're kids playing in their yards this time of day." He looked at me over the tops of his glasses as seriously as anybody has ever looked at me, so seriously that it cut through most of the sludge clogging my brain. "You better find the old guy before he kills somebody."

I took off at a run. By the time I reached Maple and turned right, the throbbing in my legs had become synchronized to my pace. It made sense that Bud would turn right onto Maple because it was the way to the driver's license office, the place he'd wanted me to take him so he could retake his eye test. And it turned out he'd left a sort of trail I could follow. In the first block I saw that two aluminum trash cans were off their concrete pads and rolling around in the culvert. A mailbox on the next block had been given a passing blow and was bent forward with its door hanging down like a tongue.

And then I came to this yellow-shingled house that's sort of a landmark in town because it has three life-sized plastic deer grazing in the yard. There were tire tracks up over the curb and through the grass, like at the Brandywines', and all three of those deer were on their backs with their plastic legs sticking straight up into the air.

"Oh man, Bud, those deer were a good six feet off the road!" I whispered.

I guess that's when Mr. Brandywine's horrifying comment became completely real to me. If Bud could take out three fake deer, couldn't he just as easily run into a *person*? Especially a *small* person or group of people too flaky to pay attention to traffic?

In a couple more blocks there was a place in the road where these wild little kids always have an afternoon game of street soccer going. I pushed my run to an all-out sprint, hoping against hope those kids had been called inside, like because one of them was having an inside birthday party or like because there had been some satellite malfunction that canceled the soap operas Janet said their parents watched all afternoon and the kids had therefore been let into their houses earlier than usual and forced to clean their rooms or something.

But all that hoping didn't work, and just as I reached that block, a pack of those soccer kids came scrambling right toward me, huge-eyed and scared-looking.

"What *happened*?" I called to them, panic cracking my voice.

"We need a grown-up!" one of them yelled as they surrounded me, grabbing my hands and my belt loops and pulling me back the way they'd come. "A car is in a yard!"

"Don't tell my mom!" one of them added, I guess to be on the safe side.

"Was anybody hurt, any of you kids?" I asked as I ran with them.

"We *never* get hurt!" one of them called up to me while a couple of his friends slugged the air belligerently to demonstrate.

I felt a surge of relief so powerful I nearly tripped over my own feet.

Then one of the others added, "The guy inside the car looks probably dead, though."

The huge boat of an Oldsmobile turned out to be parked in the middle of someone's weirdly landscaped rock garden. The car's front fender had actually come to rest on the pointed heads of a dozen or so concrete trolls. For a few crazy seconds I thought Snow White's dwarfs were trying to steal Bud's tires.

"We got a grown-up!" one of the kids with me yelled, and the other soccer kids popped up from where they'd been sitting clumped under a basketball hoop hung over a garage door across the street.

"That car shouldn't be in Jeremy's yard!" one of the girls yelled fiercely over to me, stomping her foot. "You can't drive inside grass, you know! It's against all the laws!"

"You go to *prison* for life!" some other little kid yelled in support.

"Go over with the others and tell them not to move while I check this out," I whispered gruffly to my escorts, hoping to bluff them into thinking I knew what I was doing. To my surprise, they took off at a run, obeying me.

Bud must have been heading back from the driver's license

place because the car was facing toward home. He was slumped, his forehead against the steering wheel. I threw my pack into the backseat, then jerked open the front door. Bud began drooping toward me so fast I barely bent in time to shoulder him back up. His eyes were closed and he was chalk white and covered in sweat, but at least he was breathing, taking harsh gulps of air through his mouth. Relief rushed through me, mixed with a queasy sense of urgency. I had to get him help, and fast, so I body-slammed him, grunting with the effort as I shoved him with my right hip and shoulder far enough along the wide bench seat to fit myself behind the wheel. He slumped sideways again with his head on my shoulder, exactly like we were on a date.

I grabbed the key and turned it left, then right, hoping the big car's engine wasn't flooded with gas.

The engine caught and vroomed into life. I looked to be sure the crazy little soccer kids were still across the street. "Stay out of the way!" I yelled out the window as I slammed the gearshift into reverse. The trolls were still wobbling as I bumped back down over the curb and headed in the direction of the highway.

Caspian County General Hospital was east of town. I remembered that much but couldn't picture the rest. Think, *think*. Okay, yes, it was east quite a few miles outside of town, still in Oklahoma but just this side of the Missouri state line.

"Bud?" I kept yelling, elbowing him hard. "Bud, wake up! Bud!"

No answer, but still that harsh breathing, the best sign I was going to get.

"Hang in there, Bud, we're almost there, we're almost there."

I had the Olds going eighty once we were on the highway, but still it felt like we were moving in slow motion.

Then finally I spotted the hospital, a brick building low to the ground. I was so shook up that I overshot the highway exit and had to backtrack, and when I finally got into the confusing parking lot, I couldn't see the entrance lane to the emergency room.

I was craning my neck, inching the car forward and looking desperately around, when Bud suddenly gave a rumbly series of snorts, then jerked his shoulders a couple of times and sat up straight.

"Where're we at, huh?" He lifted both hands and began smoothing his few white hairs flat against his scalp like some kind of fashionista. "Whassappening here, anyhow?"

Before I could say anything, he reached over and pulled the emergency brake handle. The car stopped with a jolt and died.

"Bud, you had a *heart* attack!" That came out way too loud, like an accusation, like I was angry. I wasn't, but I *was* pretty hysterical, I guess. "I'm trying to get you to the emergency room, Bud, before you . . . before you totally zone out and . . . and, like, *crash*!"

"Ahhh, don't be ridiculous," Bud cut in. "I just mighta had somewhat of a little event, that's all. Happens all the time. No reason to go on and on about it."

Backed-up air came out of my lungs in a sudden puff and I sagged from the shoulders, still gripping the wheel, the only control I had over this impossible situation.

"I don't blame you for not taking me to the license office

today, son," Bud muttered. "It's nothing but a nest of thieving bureaucrats. I shoulda just stayed home myself this afternoon for all the good it ended up doing me. They have no respect for the rights of a veteran to operate his own vehicle. I been driving since I was fourteen years old with—"

"—no trouble at all. I know, Bud. I know." The tendons in my shoulders were beginning to spasm, but I would not let go of that wheel. I sat there looking straight ahead, trying to figure how I could get Bud into the emergency room since I had no army with me, no police force, no SWAT team to help.

"Yeah, well, I got a map in here somewheres," Bud mentioned as he pushed his thumb against a shiny button on the dashboard. The door of the glove compartment fell open, releasing a small landslide of junk onto Bud's feet. A couple of flashlights, empty candy wrappers, and about four decks of loose playing cards. Three or four gloves, a handful of screwdrivers, and then, finally, a map of some kind.

Bud began unfolding the map and shaking out the dead insects, little ketchup packets, and old toothpicks that had been caught in its folds. While he was preoccupied, I quietly started the engine and took off the emergency brake. I'd finally noticed a small green sign with an arrow and the letters *ER* above it, and I was sneaking the car slowly toward that when Bud looked up from his map.

"Where ya think yer going?" This time, he was ferocious. "I told ya, I just had somewhat of a little event so *no hospital!*"

He jerked the emergency brake handle again. We both

pitched forward, and *this* time around when the engine died, it did it with a painful, metallic *whunk*.

"But Bud . . ." I stopped helplessly at that. Could I sprint into the hospital and sprint back out with some burly medical guys who could strong-arm him or give him some kind of shot to make him go limp so we could carry him inside?

He didn't say anything for at least a full minute, maybe longer. When he spoke, his voice was still gruff, but it was different, like he was talking more to himself than to me.

"A heart is just a pump, see. You can patch it, you can prime it, but all pumps eventually rust out. And never, ever forget, son, a man's wounds are his own."

It was the same words he'd used to get Janet to back off when she was determined to get some doctor at the clinic to fix my legs. My throat felt tight. From the corner of my eye I saw him holding his map up close to his face.

"What's the map for, Bud?" I finally asked.

"Always keep a map in your vehicle, son."

"But I mean, what are you looking for on it?"

He squinted harder at the wrinkled and splotched paper between his hands. "Thought we might go visit my old truck while we're out in this direction," he said. "It's just over into Missouri and up Highway 71 a short ways."

I stared at him in total bug-eyed shock, though he stayed engrossed in his map and didn't indicate that he noticed how his offhand suggestion had sent me reeling. I didn't want to upset him, especially since he was still the color of mashed potatoes, but there were a dozen reasons why that was a horrible idea, including that neither of us could—surprise, surprise—*drive*! I mean, of course I *had* just driven, but I'd done it mindlessly, in a white-hot emergency that left me no thinking-about-it space. Now that I *had* begun to think about it again, I figured I could maybe, just maybe, get us the twenty-minute drive home without falling completely apart. Given the choice, though, I would rather have walked the entire distance blindfolded on a tightrope strung over the highway.

"Bud? That truck may no longer exist," I pointed out, very quietly. Why would it, after somewhere around seventy years? "I think we should do some Internet research to, like, learn more about the make of truck it was and—"

He snorted, insulted. "Course it exists. Why wouldn't it?"

There were cars mounting up behind us, but I didn't dare start the ignition again.

"Bud, please, just let the emergency room people check you out, then we'll go home and turn on the game and peel potatoes for Janet to make supper and . . ."

He lowered his arms and let the map drop limply to his lap. Something about that really got to me. It was like a piece of his essential Bud-ness had collapsed in on itself.

"You know the worst thing about being old?" he muttered. "Look at me, son."

I swallowed hard and looked more directly at him.

"It's that people treat you like you're stupid just because your eyes don't work so well and your feet got no feeling. What's that got to do with brains, huh?"

It was a real question. He was clearly waiting for an answer. "Nothing, Bud."

"Yeah, okay, then. You decided to bring me here, and it was a good call, seeing as how I was unresponsive, as they say on those TV medical shows. So thanks. But now, I am responsive again and so *I* decide whether to go to the hospital, and I say no."

He faced the windshield and raised his chin a notch, set his teeth so his jawbone jutted. He painstakingly rebuttoned a place on his shirt that had gapped open, then clasped his hands together in his lap like I do at the dentist's office.

"So. Let's go home," he said without a trace of anything resembling enthusiasm. In fact, his voice held the opposite of enthusiasm. He sounded so . . . flat. So flattened.

My mouth felt dry. He was right. It *was* his decision. I started the car and forced myself not to even look over at the turn lane for the ER. At the hospital exit I signaled left and sat there waiting for traffic to clear. The pump that was my own heart somehow synchronized itself with the turn signal—*buh-BOOM, buh-BOOM, buh-BOOM.*

I glanced over at Bud. He was staring out the dirty windshield at the scruffy little browned-off cedar trees that lined the hospital parking lot like so many incurable patients.

Then suddenly I could hear Bud's thoughts. I know it sounds

strange, but I could actually *hear* them. Bud's thoughts were clear and solid, which set them completely apart from the murky workings of my own sludged-up brain.

Bud was thinking that when he got home today, he would never again have the freedom to go anywhere that he wanted to go. The big Olds would go back into the garage and he would go back into his La-Z-Boy and his license would be a thing to toss when he scoured his wallet for trash like Trey had scoured his as he searched for that lost twenty last Saturday.

Except for the Trey comparison, those were Bud's thoughts. And there was something else. Bud was telling himself to accept this, to buck up, to be a man.

The traffic cleared and I turned right. It wasn't exactly a decision, just a movement.

"Hey!" Bud jerked in the same stiff way he jerked when the Chiefs did something either unforgivable or totally fantastic.

"I owe you one, Bud, so we'll look for your truck," I mumbled as I tried to get a handle on the consequences of what I'd just done. "Janet's getting home at six thirty, though, so we don't have long. Twenty minutes, half an hour max, okay?"

"*Now* you're talking!" Bud rolled his window down and crooked his elbow outside, then relaxed back into the seat. The map began flying around the car like some huge prehistoric winged creature. "Nothing can beat the open road!" he crooned. "A day of freedom on the open highway beats a year cooped up inside four walls, know what I mean?"

I summoned a half smile for him, but I just couldn't manage

a phony nod of agreement. Both legs gave me a simultaneous stab of bright pain, and I remember it crossing my mind that everyone but Bud could surely see that the open road was nothing but a horror show.

I didn't have any idea how accurate that crazy exaggeration would turn out to be.

IX

I DROVE INTO MISSOURI in a cold clench, and by the time we reached Highway 71 and began climbing north, all the cells in my body were screaming with the effort of merely keeping the car on the road. The backs of my legs were screaming too as the plastic-covered padding of the front seat molded itself painfully around them and squeezed.

Meanwhile Bud sat grinning wide, the strong breeze from the open window spiking his few hairs. "Some fun, huh?" he kept calling across to me.

I gritted my teeth, pretending I didn't hear, using sheer willpower to stay in control. It was just crazy to put something as flimsy as a human being into something as fast as a car and then to put *that* onto a stretch of hard and treacherous asphalt. Especially when some people behind the wheel were clueless losers who didn't even *deserve* to be driving.

I had no idea where that last thought had come from, and I somehow knew I didn't *want* to know. I focused on checking the fluorescent green dial of the dashboard clock, hoping it would hurry up and give me the excellent news that twenty minutes had passed.

Finally, finally, finally that happened, twenty minutes had inched by. I'd wiped my wet palms on my jeans so much that I could feel clammy tracks on the denim clear down to my knees.

"So, Bud?" I called across to him. "It's been over twenty minutes and we're surely past where you thought your truck might be. I'm turning back at the next exit."

I held my breath, wondering what he'd have to say. I could feel the car pulling against me, veering slightly right and left, trying to ease itself from my hands. The Olds knew I had no business on the road, so surely Bud had figured that out by now as well.

Bud took the map and snapped it open. "Lemme just check something here."

I waited as long as I could stand it, then I asked, "So, do you . . . see it?"

He didn't answer. A quick sideways glance showed me that he'd dozed off, still holding up the map. "Bud!" I guess I really yelled that, and when he jerked awake, I repeated, a little more quietly but even *more* desperately, "Hey, Bud, do you *see* it?"

He blinked and peered at me. "See what?"

"Your truck, Bud! Your pickup truck! We've been traveling for thirty-seven minutes now! We agreed on twenty! Do you see what you were looking for on the map?"

Bud snorted a low laugh. "They're not about to show a pickup truck on a map, son." He grabbed my shoulder. "Listen, kid, try to relax a little bit, huh? Get back on the horse that bit you. No, on the dog that bit you. No, get back on the horse that *threw* you."

I felt something warm go into my tense right shoulder from Bud's wide, blunt-fingered hand. He was trying to get me past the awful thing that had happened, that was now clear, but I fought against relaxing like he'd advised. When you relax is when all hell breaks loose. One day you come home from first grade with a picture of a pirate you've made and you find your mother in bed and four months later she dies. You come home from school another day to find your father gone and he never comes back.

The last thing you can do is relax into safety. Just look at what happened . . . *this* time.

Bud tossed the map over his shoulder and it sailed around the backseat and finally flapped out the open window. "You gotta know when to use a map, son, and you also gotta know when to lose one," Bud said. "We'll find that truck by feel, I reckon."

I shot him an openmouthed look, too shocked to do anything else.

"Did I ever tell you about my dog, Pedro?" Bud asked, crossing his arms and chuckling. "Little crazy-looking white dog with one black ear, skinny as a rabbit. I had Pedro for all of thirteen years, then the day I started high school, I came home and Pedro was nowhere to be found. I looked for him every night for a week, but no Pedro. Looked in all his favorite haunts over and over again—in the goat pen, back behind my dad's blacksmithing shed, up under the front porch where he'd tunneled himself a nice cozy sleeping place. The night I finally decided he was gone for good, I walked behind the barn and just sat there. I loved that dog, good old ugly little dog, that Pedro."

He slapped his knee. "You know, I won more money playing poker on the troop ship going to Korea than I got in my paycheck. Don't tell Mary that! Oh no, don't tell Mary."

He got quiet for a few seconds, the heavy kind of quiet. "To this day I forget my Mary's gone," he mentioned in a soft, sad way. And then he reached across and clutched my shoulder again. "Hey, I lost my train of thought. I meant to tell you that the paperboy is coming over for dinner tonight! Yeah, Janet gave him an invite when he came in this morning. After he left, I told Janet you and me would make ourselves scarce, grab a burger someplace. So see? The later we get home, the better."

Make ourselves scarce? "Bud, the paperboy is just a fifth grader! I mean, I guess Sam might be big for his age, but you know he's only ten or eleven years old, right?"

"Who'd ya mean, Sam?" Bud asked. "This guy's name is Stephens. Henry Stephens. Knows you from the police station Saturday night. Been stopping by to check and see that you're all right, or so he says." He snickered. "*I* say he's checking out Janet, just using you and bringing in the newspaper as a coupla big fat excuses to see her."

I was boggled by all this and missed an exit where I could have turned around.

"Dad gave up farming for a while in the late 1930s and early 1940s," Bud said quietly. "It got too hard to make a living on the land, too much drought, and he took up truck-ing, though Mama and my little sister and me stayed put on the farm. Sometimes he let me go with him on a run of three or four days, to get outta my mother's hair, I suppose. He'd fall asleep driving sometimes and my job was to grab the wheel and nudge him awake again. Or sometimes he'd even take a nap back in the truck bed and I'd drive, though that wasn't until I was twelve or so, plenty able to keep the loaded rig on the road. We spent a coupla nights in jail once. Cops pulled us over and our load was confiscated. Don't know what was packed in those wooden boxes back there, all Dad knew was he was given it by a crew in Omaha. Police said it was empty bottles from a Nebraska glass factory, bound for Al Capone's illegal whiskey operation, up Chicago way. Mama was never told about that little incident. Then we got stuck on a bridge over the Mississippi once when we were overloaded with ripe watermelons, down in the Missouri bootheel. They had to gather up a bunch of farmers and horses to—"

"Wait, wait, wait! You were involved with bootleg whiskey, Bud?"

"Nah, just the bottles. And then once Dad and I skidded right off the road in heavy rain near Des Moines and . . ."

I began remembering Bud telling Trey and me stories like this one back when we were in third grade while we sprawled on the blue oval carpet over by Bud's chair with sofa cushions under our chins and just kept listening right through the shows we'd meant to watch. Janet let us bring food in there, and Ding

Dongs became our special story-listening food, with Twinkies a close second. . . .

"Well, we ended up waiting overnight for the truck to get fixed, so we took in quite a peep show at a carnival that was passing through. That is, Dad bought a ticket and went in and I waited outside as I was told to do until a couple of boys that were sneaking in under the back side of the tent beckoned for me to join them, and oh boy, did *I* get an eyeful!"

Bud talked on, and I felt my grip on the wheel get both more relaxed and firmer. I'd forgotten how Bud telling you his life had been like watching the kind of movie that makes you forget where you are and even *who* you are for a welcome while.

But suddenly the traffic grew much heavier and one of those green highway signs floated by—*Raytown, 6 miles.* How could we be nearing the suburbs of Kansas City?

Panic dropped on me again like it'd been stuck to the ceiling of the car.

"I can't do this, Bud," I wheezed. "Look at me. I'm shaking so hard I can't grip the wheel! I'm not kidding, I don't know how we got so far from home and I . . . I can't drive clear back from here, there's absolutely no way!"

"Just *once* in my lifetime I'd like to see them Chiefs lose to my face," Bud mentioned.

Then he turned to look directly at me. "Kid, you're right, you're not looking so good. Pull over awhile, why doncha? Eat a candy bar or something. Get your second wind."

I swung out of traffic and onto the wide gravel shoulder,

where I turned off the ignition and collapsed with my forehead against the steering wheel. I heard Bud rummaging in the glove compartment, and after a couple of minutes he poked my arm with what turned out to be most of a Milky Way bar, its chocolate gone white with age.

It was rock hard and what Janet would call "questionable," but I ate it anyway, pretty much inhaled it. And while I gobbled that ancient candy bar, Bud closed his eyes, slouched back with his head against his seat, and told a different sort of story.

"There'd been heavy artillery fire on us for days," he began in a raspy whisper. "We three were sheltered together in a trench cut through a minefield we'd cleared the week before. Tom Gulliver—this was my buddy from back on the farm—Tom Gulliver and me and a city boy named Clark Jackson who played good poker. We three shared that shallow space there in that Korean mud, crouched down with our carbines and grenades at the ready but with the enemy hid from sight.

"We were cracking every kind of joke, hunkered down with our helmets pulled low on our foreheads and so scared we couldn't think. Others in our platoon were somewhere along the length of the trench. We'd hear 'em laughing at their own forms of jokes, but it was dark by then, too dark to see what was what or who was where. So, all right, in comes your worst nightmare, a mortar blast, tore a big hole in Clark and killed him instant like. Tore off Tommy's legs and he died later, raving, no more'n ten feet from me, though I couldn't get to him through the smoking rubble since I myself was laid open from hip to shoulder. I talked to Tommy all through the night, mostly about his sweetheart from back in Nebraska, his fine horse he was fixing to rodeo with when he got out of the army, his grandma's applesauce cake he was always going on about.

"Then Tommy got suddenly quiet just as dawn was breaking. When the strong light of day finally reached into that trench, I gritted my teeth and hoisted myself up and saw Tommy's body, lying there mangled and dusty, and kneeling beside him was . . . was . . ."

He stopped for so long that I finally clutched his shoulder and leaned over to search his face. He looked at me, or looked right *through* me, with an expression impossible to describe. He was seeing something from the past, or from the future, or maybe both. Seeing it with fear or longing. Fear *and* longing, combined?

"*Who* was kneeling beside Tommy, Bud?" I asked in a whisper.

He didn't answer at first, then he whispered, "It was . . . her. You know. *Her.*"

Bud closed his eyes and I jerked my jacket from my backpack and was folding it into a sort of lumpy pillow for his neck when a huge wave of dizziness rolled through me. For a second or two I assumed it was that candy bar, but then I had the weird sensation of things spinning completely out of my control, of time and space going haywire.

A metallic creaking started up somewhere outside the car. I stuck my head out the window to figure out where it was coming from and saw a huge green sign hanging over the highway and rocking in a sudden gust of wind. Had it even *been* there before?

In large, glistening reflective letters it read *Arrowhead Stadium, take next exit.*

The wind stopped as quickly as it had come up. Even the tiniest sunflowers along the highway quit dancing and froze. But that sign still bucked and twisted like a bronco in the still air. I watched it and felt my insides grow slowly cold in the same way they did when I woke at night and listened, helplessly, to Trey's chattering rock.

Whether you understand them or not, messages are messages. We hadn't gotten off the highway in this spot, under this particular sign, by simple accident. *Take next exit.* It was like someone "up there" was using a green tablet provided by the Highway Department to give me a command, or possibly just a very strong suggestion. Either way, in spite of my being messed up and Bud being sick and our being so far away from home already and neither of us having any business driving in the first place, who was I to argue? Enormous signs don't flop around in the air all on their own and for no reason.

"Hey, Bud?" I heard myself whisper. "If . . . if you want to see the Chiefs play, why not, since we're here at the turnoff to the stadium. You're buying the hot dogs, though, right? That was the deal you gave me last Sunday."

Bud's eyes popped open and he straightened in his seat and clapped. "Yeah, kid, *now* you're talking! Get this buggy moving or we'll miss the kickoff!"

I started the car, took the exit, and zigged, white-knuckled and nauseated, through city traffic. The other drivers seemed willing to get out of my way, and we got tickets easily enough at the stadium gate, probably because the team had been slumping. Or maybe as a reward from the crazy universe for Bud's equally crazy thirty-year fandom.

Whatever, the Chiefs broke a six-game losing streak with a squeaker over the Raiders that evening. Bud was justifiably cocky, taking all the credit, slapping all the other wildly ecstatic fans on the back as we made our way to the parking lot.

We found the car easily, huge and unique as it was, and I managed to maneuver it out of the worst of the stadium traffic without slamming into anything. Again, that was probably because everybody got out of my way. I was pretty terrified driving in the dusk. It seemed even chancier than broad daylight had been, like any number of things could come at you from the shadows, trucks and motorcycles and so forth. Only the energy jolt from the three hot dogs and two large sodas I'd gulped kept me steady enough to successfully backtrack so that eventually the Highway 71 sign loomed like a great and welcome gift out of the twilit fog just ahead of us.

I let out a long, shaky breath. "Okay, Bud, we made it!" We were still a good three hours from home, but the trickiest part was done. Once we were on 71, I'd become part of the herd of cars rushing straight south, no complications. "We oughta stop pretty soon and give Janet a call or she'll be—"

"Watchit, watchit, watchit!" Bud suddenly yelled. "Right

there, right there! You're about to miss your exit! Turn, boy, *turn*!"

And I *knew* that the exit to 71 south was still most of a mile down the road. I'd just read that on the sign, so I *knew* it! Yet when someone like Bud is screaming in your ear, you just have time to think how awful it'd be if you *did* miss your exit. You *don't* have time to think about arguing or even to think about what you're doing, you just, basically, have time to picture missing your exit like Bud is screaming that you're about to do and then in the half second left, you, well, react.

I swung the wheel to the right and squealed off the highway and onto the exit ramp. I didn't even have time to signal and the guy right behind me laid on his horn.

When we were halfway down that long ramp, I could see another one of those green signs posted above the road we were merging onto. *Highway 71 North to Omaha.*

We were heading in the totally wrong direction, going toward Nebraska, not Oklahoma, and who knew how or where I'd be able to get turned around to go back?

"Watchit, watchit, watchit!" Bud yelled again.

I whipped my attention from that sign back to the ramp we were sailing down, and instantly my heart convulsed into a tight ball of panic. There was someone in the middle of the road, right straight ahead of us!

I hit the brake so hard that the Olds sashayed left and right and shrieked and groaned and finally came to a rocking stop mere feet from what turned out to be a small girl in red cowboy boots with a black motorcycle jacket tied by the arms around her waist.

She was calmly sitting on a huge green backpack with her left ankle propped on her right knee, jiggling her left boot as though she was *bored* or something! The wind was spiking her short, choppy blue hair and she began chewing her right thumbnail as she stared back at me through the dirty windshield. She looked to be about fifteen, maybe sixteen. Or she could have been older, just small-boned and scrappy.

I couldn't read her expression, but it was definitely weird. It was like she had *no* expression, just looked at me with a blank face, this when she had nearly become roadkill, nearly been smashed as flat as some nocturnal beast without the sense to get out of the way of a huge piece of unstoppable machinery.

I couldn't breathe and my hands were rubber on the wheel. "Bud . . . I . . . I didn't even *see* her!" I fought down a couple more gulps of air and added, "She . . . she wasn't sitting there two seconds before, I swear it! And then she just . . . she just . . . was."

My hands were cramping and my knees felt loose.

"Things loom up fast on the highway, son," Bud whispered, then he actually chuckled. By the eerie green light of the instrument panel I could make out the strangest goofy smile on his normally granite face.

X

STEAM BURST from under the hood and the blue-haired girl just sat casually jiggling her foot and staring at me through that thick haze, still with that blank look on her doll-like pale face. Right about then I figured out she wasn't blinking. That was what made her expression seem so strange. She never, ever blinked!

She finally stood and stretched, gave a yank to the frayed cuffs of her jacket to pull it tighter around her waist, then shouldered her pack and sauntered slowly toward the car, casually wiping her wet thumb on the short strip of black fabric that passed for her skirt.

"She must be hitching, Bud, probably trying to get a ride to Omaha. Soon as I find a place to turn around, we'll be going the opposite direction she wants to go."

I began rolling down my window to tell *her* that same thing.

Bud reached across and clutched my shoulder, really gave it some grip.

"Don't ever leave a lady stranded on the highway, son," he said, softly but sternly.

"But Bud . . ." That's as far as I got before I was interrupted by the noise of highway traffic as the back door jerked open and the strange girl and her posse of damp night shadows all slipped into the Oldsmobile with us.

Things instantly went murky. I mean, sure, it had been dusky before, but it hadn't yet gone authentically dark. The air had contained enough light for me to clearly see Bud sitting there with his knees wide apart and his arms crossed. The green glow from the instrument panel had turned the hairs on his arms to a green fuzz, but his outline beneath that fuzz had been plenty solid.

Suddenly, though, when *she* got in, everything got less distinct and seemed sort of smudged together so you didn't know where one thing stopped and another thing began. My hands seemed to be growing from the steering wheel. Bud seemed to be melting into the seat. That sort of thing.

I straightened the rearview mirror and watched her yank her overloaded pack in after her like a reluctant pet, then she slammed the door and everything in back was lost to my sight except for her huge, luminous eyes. They seemed to float back there, disembodied.

A sickeningly sweet smell wafted up to us. Bud's head flopped back against the yellowed white vinyl that protected the top of the seat and staggered snores started coming from his direction.

"Uh, listen," I told her reflection, trying to sound no-nonsense. "You need a different ride. We'll be getting off at the next exit to head south, to Oklahoma."

She scooted up to perch on the edge of her seat with her face only nine or ten inches from my shoulder. She blew a huge grape bubble, broke it and peeled the edges off her nose, sucked the whole mess back into her mouth, then gave the whole rank gob a couple of openmouthed smacks before taking it out and planting it behind her ear.

"Got a light?" she asked.

She was holding a bent cigarette between her thumb and index finger. I opened my mouth to tell her that Bud had a bum heart and she couldn't smoke, but those words didn't happen. Instead, I just sat there and watched as my hand dug Trey's green Bic lighter from my jeans pocket and handed it back to her.

She snatched it and held it up between us. "Six!" she announced cheerfully, bouncing on her seat like a child. She clicked Trey's lighter one, two, three, four, five times. *Whoosh!* On the sixth, it lit. I could feel its heat on the rim of my ear.

"Fire is so darn hot, isn't it?" She giggled, then snorted, then giggled again, holding that flame even closer to my flesh.

I ducked left. "Hey!" The rim of my ear felt scorched.

I thrust my hand over my shoulder for the lighter, hoping all the while that my fingers weren't trembling. It was time she quit horsing around with her sickening gum and her nasty cigs and just got herself and her pack out of Bud's car.

"You're no fun." She gave me a quick pouty look, then lit up. When the flame was snuffed she threw the Bic onto my palm, then shoved hard with her boots against my seat to jettison herself backward. In the rearview mirror I saw those backseat shadows gathering close around her like long-lost children. Soon she was again nothing but unblinking, glowing eyes with a moving orange dot below them that was the burning tip of her cigarette.

"You're *not* going with us," I told her again. I was trying to make that an angry order, but the words came out of me in something nearing a whimper.

She gave a bored sigh. "Oh, don't be silly, of course I am. I'll drive, but you're a quart low on oil so you might as well go ahead and merge while I enjoy my cig. Half a mile on there's an exit. Take it and turn right and there'll be a gas station at the top of the hill. In the parking lot you'll see an old Jeep Cherokee with a swan hood ornament and a ladder on top. Pull up at the empty pump behind it."

My head suddenly felt like it was being crushed in a vise. I gripped the wheel, then watched myself reach to turn the key. My foot was numb as a lifeless club as I gave Bud's car several big gulps of gas and we lurched the rest of the way down the ramp.

I didn't know or care if other cars were coming in my lane as I merged.

And the next thing I remember is pulling into a place called Tom's Snatch and Grab.

Bud sort of woke up when I stopped the car behind this

massive old Jeep. Still in a half-daze, I read one of its many bumper stickers. *DIRT-LOVING TREE HUGGERS!*

"Whatzit? Where we at, huh?" Bud asked.

The hitchhiker girl unlatched her door and used her boots to push it wide. "We desperately need a quart of oil, Bud, and guess what? They've got banana Popsicles at this place! The kind that break in the middle!" She took off for the convenience store, zigzagging around the cars and gas pumps that crowded the busy parking lot.

"I think she hypnotized me or something and, like, *made* me drive here," I muttered, rubbing my neck. "Bud, she called you by name. You don't . . . you don't *know* her, do you? I mean, you *couldn't* know her, that's insane."

"Yeah, well," Bud more or less answered in this dreamy way. "Better pop the hood."

I turned to him, frowning. "No, Bud, we absolutely need to leave her here! There's plenty of traffic at this place for her to catch a ride, and we've *gotta* get *home.*"

She rapped on the window behind my head. "Pop the hood!" she yelled.

My heart nearly exploded with the shock of that. There was no way she could be back out here with that oil already, but there she was, pulling a big green plastic Quaker State container from inside her jacket as she skipped like a child to the front of the car.

"Heh, heh," Bud laughed in that soft, un-Bud-like way.

I groped under the dashboard and found the latch, and the

hood came unhooked with a clank. She was just propping it open as I jumped from the car to take over the job, but as I reached the front, the big hood slammed down again with such righteous force that if I'd had another second to lean forward, it would surely have beheaded me.

How could she *possibly* have added that oil so quick? She'd had, what? Five seconds?

"Hey, get back in the car!" she yelled, wiping her hands on my sleeve as she zipped past me. She tossed the empty oil container into a trash barrel over by the gas pumps, a twenty-foot swish any of the Lakers would have envied. Then she slipped through the door I'd left open and slid beneath the wheel, and I heard the big engine thrum to life.

A guy burst from the store and began angrily jabbing the air with both index fingers. "Somebody stop that car!" he yelled. "She's a thief! Somebody get the license number of that big Olds while I call the police!"

The crazy hitchhiker girl gave a wicked giggle and gunned it. Luckily she'd left the back door open, and I had one split second to dive into the backseat as she swerved around the big Jeep, which, sure enough, had a swan hood ornament. Silver lettering on its front door read *Truehart Organic Farm* and the people inside gave us some goofy smiles and flashed us the peace sign as we sailed past.

The girl began driving at warp speed and head-banging to some Slipknot she'd summoned up on the radio while Bud held a banana Popsicle against the dashboard, karate-chopping it.

When it broke, he held one half over his shoulder, offering it to me.

"That's thoughtful of you, Bud," I heard the crazy hitchhiker yell above her music. "But he doesn't want a taste of your Popsicle. I can tell from the vibe he's sending out that what he *wants* is a taste of oblivion."

Had I heard those crazy sentences right? I was suddenly breathless and disoriented. I felt myself listing to the side until my head came to rest on the crazy hitchhiker's backpack. It smelled like that grape bubble gum. But beneath that sickening sweetness, it smelled like old beat-up canvas, like my camping tent, the one Steve and Zero and Trey and I sometimes took to the lake on weekends when Zero's uncle lent us his boat.

I slid down, down, down into a memory as deep, dark, and chilly as the water at Thunderbird Lake on any October weekend. The four of us were in the boat, racing the wind with the throttle wide open. The motor was too loud to hear anything anybody tried to yell to the others, but we were all whooping and hollering and yelling things to each other anyway. We couldn't keep our mouths shut once the boat was going full throttle like that, couldn't keep from yelling out nothing in particular, couldn't keep from shrieking and laughing, even though our teeth ached with the icy wind and our open mouths kept filling with fish-smelling lake spray.

Zero and Steve were in the two bucket seats up front. Steve was at the wheel, and he kept doubling us back and spinning the boat in tight circles so that the hull whapped hard and rhythmically over the waves we'd just made, bouncing us around like a bucking horse. It was a favorite in Zero's list of boat thrills, and his hyena laugh was shrill enough to cut through the noise of the motor and float on the wet wind. At one point a massive wave smacked us a good one and we were completely drenched—hair, T-shirts, jeans, and bare feet. We thought that was hilariously funny and slapped each other on the backs.

I nuzzled farther into that old canvas smell and felt happy. The memory or dream went on and on like that, just like the hours had gone on and on those afternoons we'd had the boat and the freedom of a lake made empty by water too cold for normal people.

"This is great!" Trey yelled across to me. He was sitting on the floor of the boat, there in the back. I was sitting across from him, also on the floor, leaning against the side of the boat with my arms spread along the top rim. I could read Trey's lips, even with his red hair blowing across his face. "Let's do this forever, Tucker, my *man*!"

I nodded hard and smiled like a lunatic. My face was stretched from grinning, from all that water hitting it, from yelling and yelling nothing that was important enough for you to wonder if it was heard, which it never, ever was.

The sun gradually trailed through the sky without our noticing until we were all shivering pretty bad, which made us reluctantly realize that night was edging in.

"Any of y'all wanta ski today?" Steve yelled back to us. "Trey? Tuck? It's getting colder, guys. We better ski if we're goin' to."

Nobody answered him. We seldom got around to skiing, not in October with the lake all ours and the water so cold and the boat so fast with no other boats in its way.

"It's getting colder, guys," he repeated, and turned around to Trey and me with his blond hair wind-wrecked and wild. "It's getting a *lot* . . . colder."

Steve raised one sunburned hand to shove his hair back and beneath it was . . . nothing. Where his handsome face should have been there was only black nothingness.

Zero gave his hyena laugh again and when he turned toward us, his long tangled dreads blew across nothingness as hollow and infinite as Steve's nothingness had been.

And then, Trey called my name and I had no choice, I had to turn to him. . . .

I came awake in a cold sweat and drew in a quick breath. It took me a good ten hammering heartbeats to figure out I was still in the backseat of Bud's car, only now the big windows framed trapezoids of silver light. It was morning, around dawn.

The gold diamond-patterned ceiling of the Olds looked like a coffin lid above me, and I jerked to a sit and rubbed my face, hard, with both hands. My legs came awake and sent raw pain sizzling through me. When I saw I was alone in the car, I let out a couple of good, long groans before settling in to focus on mentally blocking some of that pain. The hitchhiker must have driven to where she was going and then vamoosed, leaving Bud to drive on. But where had we ended up, and where *was* Bud?

I unlatched the door and shoved my shoulder hard against

it. When it rocked open, my ears filled with the coyote howl of hard, straight wind. I swung my legs slowly and painfully out of the car and lifted myself into tall grass, hip high.

But no, it wasn't grass, it was wheat, lots and lots of *wheat,* like they grow by the mile in states like Kansas. I slogged out a few feet and turned in a slow circle with my hands on my head. I saw nothing but a vast ocean of wildly blowing grain— no utility lines, no people, no nothing for what must have been miles and miles around. There wasn't even a road we could have driven in on, just the car and me.

It could have been two hundred years ago. Or it could have been two hundred years in the future and I was the last person left after global warming had taken its best shot.

And then, right at the end of my full-circle tour, I saw the house. It was a two-story ruin perched on a small hill. It had an attic with a round window that gave me the creepy feeling that I was being stared at. The house seemed to drift on this ocean of wheat like a rattletrap ship riding the crest of a golden wave.

Bud had to be inside. There was nowhere else he could be.

I grabbed my pack from the floor of the car. The keys were still hanging from the ignition switch and I pocketed them. I took off at a fast lope toward the house. My legs protested in the most extreme way at first, but just like yesterday, the pain became a slight bit easier to deal with when I'd hit my stride and it pulsed in time with my pace.

"Bud!" I called when I figured I was near enough for him to

hear above the wind. "Bud, you in there? Bud! Wake up and get out here, we gotta get *home*!"

"Tell me the honest truth, Tucker Graysten. Do I look good with blue hair or is it too harsh for my delicate features? Do you think I should go with, say, raspberry?"

I stopped in my tracks, every nerve in my body gone taut with dread. Sometimes you believe what you want to believe, and I'd believed she was gone, that she'd reached her destination or left the car to get another ride or take a bus or hoof it or something.

But no such luck. I turned in the direction of her voice. She was over to my left maybe twenty feet, sitting on the ground with only her fluorescent hair, heart-shaped face, and skinny white neck visible above the wheat. I doubt I'd have seen her at all if she hadn't called out to me. But then I realized she *hadn't* called out, and that's why my skin was suddenly crawling. Her words had been a frustrated, mumbled gripe about her hair like girls are always making when they want you to tell them they look really good just the way they are.

So why *had* I heard her above the banshee howl of the wind?

I took some skulking strides in her direction, leaving myself plenty of escape room in case she tried to play some weird mind game with me like she had in the car last night. She was sitting in a circle of flattened wheat, a tiny version of Steve's English crop circle. She was rummaging wildly through that overstuffed pack of hers, and as I watched, she eased out a mirror the size of a dinner plate and began frowning at herself in it, pulling up handfuls of her hair for her own inspection and wrinkling her nose at her reflection.

I turned quietly back toward the house, hoping she was so absorbed with her crazy appearance that she'd forgotten all about me. Maybe I even tiptoed, lame as that sounds. I remember I harbored a slight, idiotic hope that now she'd just wander away and be gone by the time I woke Bud and got him into the car.

"What're we doing here anyhow, Tucker Graysten?" she grumbled to my back.

An overwhelming sense of doom shot through me like a virus. I reminded myself that *she'd* been the one at the wheel last night, not me. But her stupid question had somehow given me the weird feeling that I *did* know more than I knew that I knew.

I forced myself to turn and face her. "I have no clue what *you're* doing here," I called. "I mean, I don't know why *you* were sitting in the middle of the road last night. But Bud and I were headed back to Oklahoma after a Chiefs game when you got in the car. Janet, my stepmother, Bud's daughter, probably called the police when we didn't make it home last night. I wouldn't be surprised to see the cops pull up at any time."

Let *her* be the jittery one for a change. Hitchhiking on the interstate *was* illegal.

But she just smirked. "That's not what I meant and you know it, Tucker Graysten."

That's not what I meant and you know it. How could she expect me to even *know* what I knew? I couldn't get anything straight when everything she said was so crazy.

The wind suddenly snatched her by her spiky hair and pulled her to the side so roughly she had to dig in hard with the heels of her cowboy boots to keep from being blown away. She was so small, bird-boned, and she looked very childlike with her white, knobby knees. I'd have to say she was pretty, but in a sharp-edged, willful way.

"What's so funny?" she yelled, glowering at me as she struggled to regain her balance.

I didn't think I'd laughed, and even if I had, it was just a nervous reaction. The last time I'd *authentically* laughed was when Steve and Zero and Trey and I were driving from Speed Mart to the zinc mine fields with the Mustang's top down and the October moon rising and no clue in the world of what was about to happen.

The memory was like a stomach punch. "Nothing's funny," I barely managed to get out. My guts had suddenly clenched into a raw knot, and there she sat staring with wide-eyed interest at me like I was some science experiment she was conducting. Yes, conducting—I would have sworn that sickening memory had been a little gift from her, just like the nightmare dream in the car last night had been.

I ordered myself to get a grip. The canvas smell of her pack had triggered that dream, not her personally. I noticed that gob of grape gum still stuck like a fungus behind her left ear. It was more than I could handle, and I doubled over and retched.

"Poor baby, maybe you're dying?" She giggled and shrugged, then began fishing ruthlessly through the pockets of her motorcycle jacket, chewing her bottom lip in concentration. She finally came up with half a crushed cigarette and held it between two bitten-to-the-quick purple fingernails as she fished with her other hand, probably for a match, all the while bracing herself against the wind with her heels dug in deep.

I took Trey's green lighter from my pocket and threw it across to her. "I'm going up to that house to wake Bud," I muttered, but I didn't move to do that.

She snatched the lighter from the air, looking surprised. "You'd part with this?"

I'd meant to lend it to her again like I had last night in the car. I wanted it back, of course I did, but for some reason I couldn't bring myself to say so.

She grinned that jack-o'-lantern grin of hers that was too wide for her small, sharp face. "You want it back," she accused. "I'll tell you what. Let's play a game! I'll trade you something for it."

I shook my head. "I've only got Bud's keys, and you're *not* getting those."

She held the lighter out in front of her. "Nine," she announced. She clicked it one, two, three, four, five, six, seven, eight times. *Fwoom!*—on the ninth, it lit.

I was surprised the lighter had fired in this wind, let alone on her count. The way she could predict its flare was eerily like what I had tried to do after Trey had seemed so sarcastic in my hoop house dream. But I was getting used to her cheap tricks and outrageous predictions. And even if she *could* somehow manipulate the information in my dreams and memories, that also could have some gimmick to it, like when those TV psychics appear to know everything about people's love lives, their dead dogs, et cetera.

Still, there was something more intense I had trouble explaining to myself. It was the sense of danger I felt when she got quiet, like right then, smoking. It was as if something big was silently rolling toward me and I couldn't run from its invisible path.

"I'm going up to wake Bud," I repeated, and again, I didn't move a muscle. This time, though, it felt more like I *couldn't* move.

"You *can't* go inside that house until we play our *game*, Tucker!" She pushed her bottom lip into a pout. "You have to *give* me something in exchange for this lighter!"

Her skin was as pale as her cigarette smoke. She seemed made from the dawn mist that was suddenly rising from the wheat, making everything clammy and cold.

"I told you," I repeated, "you're *not* getting Bud's keys."

"You don't even *have* Bud's keys, I've got them," she mentioned as she crushed her cigarette butt with her heel. "You *have* got something else, though. In the back right pocket of your jeans? Give me *that* and I'll give you the lighter."

I suddenly felt a small circle of heat in the pocket she'd mentioned. It was that obolus thing Mrs. Beetlebaum had given me. I'd forgotten all about it.

My throat went dry. "You *couldn't* have Bud's keys." I thrust cold fingers deep into the pocket where I'd dumped them not fifteen minutes before. Empty.

"Tucker? *Yoo*-hoo!" she sang out. "Oh, *Tuck*-er."

She had Bud's key ring around her left index finger and was casually twirling it while she frowned into her big mirror again. "Tell me the truth. Blue? Or raspberry."

"Give me back those keys." I wanted the heat of my righteous anger to burn through the layer of fear that coated my throat, but that wasn't working. The fear was thickening instead, becoming suffocating so my voice was a squawk. "Bud *gave* those keys to *me*."

Without those keys we could be here forever. She'd probably seen the outline of the obolus in my pocket, thought it was a half dollar or even a silver dollar or something, and now lusted after the cigs she thought it would help her buy. I was tempted to hold up the coin and tell her I'd trade her, but not for the Bic, for the keys. Then I remembered how Mrs. Beetlebaum had gone on and on, warning me not to take it from my pocket. That must mean it was valuable, old as it was, and it wasn't mine to lose. Mrs. B. had just lent it to me for some teachery reason I hadn't gotten straight.

I wanted *so much* to taunt the vain and crazy hitchhiker right then, to ask her why she didn't just use her flimsy amateur magic to *take* what was in my back pocket, like she'd taken the keys. Didn't the rules of this criminal game of hers allow you to steal more than one thing from an innocent bystander at a time?

I didn't do that, though. You don't poke a stick at a scorpion.

"Just like you say," she suddenly admitted with a sigh, "Bud gave these keys to you, right after the funeral. Uh, funerals. But you gave them back to him, remember? That is, you left them behind when you sneaked out of the house at the crack of dawn the next morning. That was a good call, though, leaving them behind like that. You're right, you shouldn't be driving, Tucker Graysten. You almost ran over me last night, remember? Talk about white-knuckle, last-second braking! Yeeow! And you have no idea how awful you look."

She tossed the keys into her pack, then sailed her mirror like a Frisbee across to me. I tried to sidestep and let it sail on by, but from some childhood instinct my hand reached and caught it. I let it dangle from my fingers, though, unused and unwelcome.

"Take a good look," she said, and her voice suddenly seemed much lower, the voice not of a flighty young girl but of . . . something else, something not to be disobeyed.

XI

I WATCHED MY HAND hold up the mirror. Three deep cuts from the vents of Trey's locker ran clear across my forehead, and blood from those was matted in my hair and crusted on the stubbly skin of my unshaven face. My eyebrows were singed to a frizz in places. My eyelashes were mostly gone, and the lids beneath where they'd grown were now angry red. Purple hollows had set in under my cheekbones, my lips were cracked, and my eyes were shot with red and had a strange, haunted look about them.

Someone I didn't even know had crawled in and taken up residence in me.

"And beneath those jeans your *legs* are an absolute *mess*," she pointed out, rolling her eyes. "As recently as a hundred years ago people routinely died of blood poisoning from open wounds like that. Antibiotics are wonderful things, Tucker Graysten. Get a *clue!*"

"How did you . . . how *could* you . . ." Even Bud didn't know how bad my legs were.

She took the time to chew off a ragged bit of thumbnail, then gave a sigh of disgust with herself as she shook her hand in the air. "How'd I know about the legs? I *read* you, that's how. Last night, right before I got in your car? I know your whole story, Tucker. Trey picking you up at the curb last Saturday afternoon like he'd done probably a thousand times before, the borrowed ID, your first two beers and then the one Zero gave you, bailing out of the Mustang, puking in the ditch, sliding down the bluff, and everything that's happened to you since, at school and at home and at the funeral. I even know you were the careful one among those friends of yours, the guy who took care of everybody else, the cook and the lookout and the person who kept track of Trey's lost stuff, but I *still* don't know what we're *doing* here, which means you're hiding some detail, Tucker. Some sliver of truth is too far embedded in your soul for you to reach it."

I took some deep breaths and tried to concentrate on the pain in my legs so I could block her insanity. Maybe Bud had told her a bunch of that stuff she knew. Or maybe I'd talked in my sleep. Who cared how she'd got her information? She was just plain nuts, and the important thing was for us to get far away from her.

"I'm going up to that house to wake Bud," I said for the third time. My teeth were chattering so hard I tasted blood. "We're not going your way. You should go back to the main road and try for another ride."

I started toward the house again, but after a couple of steps, my legs just locked.

I whirled to face her and found I could move just fine, but only in her direction.

"What . . . are you *doing* to me?"

She gave me a puzzled look. "I'm not *doing* anything to you, Tucker Graysten. I just need you to tell me why we're here. You called me last night, and I have to admit I came in a hurry because I could smell money on you, which is sooo rare these days. I mean, they aren't making those coins hundreds of years ago, and since there are so few of them around now it's absolutely thrilling when I get paid. Usually I have to get by on, well, nothing, no payment at all, which is one of the many ways my boss is cutting corners these days. Trust me, I'd love to just grab that coin, throw you into the car, and get back behind the wheel to take you where your infected legs and your weirdness the past few days *and* your horrible driving last night tell me you want to go.

But there's something missing from your story, some little poison detail. I always want my pickups to be able to state in clear terms their own reasons for calling me, especially when they're only seventeen. It's not that you won't tell *me* why you called, it's that you won't tell *you*."

Her voice was coming from far away, echoing in my head.

"I . . . I *didn't* call you . . ." I pushed out. "You just . . . *appeared* there on the exit ramp when Bud and I were on our way back to Oklahoma from—"

"There oughta be one of those iron water pumps around here someplace," she murmured. She got to her feet and began squinting toward the house. "Yes! There it is, over on that old well curb by the kitchen garden."

"And whuh . . . what do you mean *embedded*?"

She whipped around quick as a snake and fastened me with her eyes, which suddenly were awful. Had her pupils become spirals, like the dog's? Could you buy contact lenses that did that?

"Embedded, Tucker," she whispered. "Buried so deep that recalling that little detail will be like pulling a knife from your heart. You'll bleed, maybe even to death. But whether you know it or not, you *called* me and then you picked me up, so find that piece of the story you've embedded in your soul, pull it out, let it bleed, and whatever happens, happens. I mean, I'm *here* now, so you're wasting my valuable time until you do that."

I stumbled backward, desperate to get away from her. "I . . . didn't pick you up. Bud . . . Bud was the one who picked you up. I wanted to leave you."

"You *both* picked me up." She yawned and stretched, then scratched her hair into lopsided tufts. "If anybody knows himself, it's Bud. So if you're not ready to know *your*self, then *I'm* getting started coloring this hair."

She threw Trey's lighter into her pack, then eased a hot pink squeeze bottle out of it. She turned to trek toward the old iron water pump that was framed like a hook-necked animal against the distant sky.

The wheat seemed to open a path for her. I rubbed my eyes, and when I looked at her again, she'd stopped and turned back toward me with her hand on her hip.

"I almost forgot," she called. "If you're bound and determined to see Bud, I gotta call Cherry Berry. Bud is at the point where . . . well, let's just say he's being guarded."

She tucked the bottle under her arm, put her two pinkie fingers between her lips, and produced the sort of piercing whistle I'm pretty sure can break glass.

A shadow suddenly darkened the grain. I looked to the sky but was too sun-dazzled to see anything except a huge shape up there, probably some winged predator, maybe a giant eagle or a clot of three or four buzzards.

Then the shadow grew sharper and darker and the black dog dropped out of the sky and into the wheat not four feet in front of me! He sat up on his haunches, staring at me with all three tongues lolling in big doggy smiles.

I opened my mouth, then stood there speechless, looking from the dog to the weird hitchhiker and back. "So this is—this is *your* dog?" I finally managed to stammer.

The girl started shaking that big pink bottle, looking peeved at the delay.

"Nah, we're just co-workers. He's got a tiny bit of seniority on me."

The dog turned one head toward her and set up a little whimper-whine. She rolled her eyes, then drew the lighter from her pack and looked at it wistfully.

"Cherry Berry says I have to give this back. He likes you. That's why he brought you Trey's green lighter in the first place."

She threw it to me, and I caught and pocketed it. "He dug it up across the street from my house," I muttered quietly, rubbing my forehead. Had I told her it had been Trey's?

She snorted. "Don't make me laugh. CB brought Trey's lighter from a *lot* farther away than that. He probably thought it might help solve this little *problem* of yours."

Without waiting for my response, which would have been utter confusion, she turned and headed toward the pump again. The wheat slammed like an iron gate behind her.

The dog meanwhile sat quivering in every muscle, then bounded right up into the air.

I watched him swoop up the hill, do a flyby of the house, then circle twice around the roof. He finally did a four-point clumsy landing on the porch, where he regained his balance and stood facing, facing, facing me, eagerly waiting for me to join him.

I swallowed hard and finally resumed my own hike up the hill, breathing deep, which I hoped was a way to keep panic from getting the best of you.

I still thought, or I guess I mean I *hoped,* the weird girl was simply insane.

But something about seeing that flying dog with his gangly legs hanging so loose and his big floppy ears tossing in the wind had made me admit to myself that when I reached that big black dog that reminded me a little of Ringo, I wouldn't be joining a him.

I would be joining an *it.*

By the time I reached the porch steps, the dog was chasing

its tail in close circles like dogs do when they're especially eager to get going. I made doggy small talk, said it was a good dog and so forth, and when I was balanced on the rickety floor of the porch itself, I even went down in a crouch at the dog's level to show I was its friend.

I stopped short of reaching out to scratch its ears, though. I wouldn't say I was squeamish, not exactly. Just off-balance, like I was around the girl. In fact, I had the sudden thought that I wouldn't have wanted to touch *her* either.

"Is Bud inside?" I asked the dog, and in answer it turned all three heads toward the front door, which was banging in the wind. I caught it and held it still and open a few inches and the dog slid through and disappeared into the gloom inside the house.

I followed but stopped just over the threshold to adjust my eyes to the sad and murky shadows of what must have once been the kitchen of the place. Wooden cupboards sagged against the walls, so shrouded with cobwebs they looked like mummies. Shards of broken glassware studded the floor—the handle of a cup, half a flowered plate. I made out a rusted pump bolted to the edge of a large sink, its white porcelain fuzzed with mold. A mouse skittered from the spout of an overturned teapot.

I took a breath and called, "Hey, Bud, you awake? We gotta hit the road!"

I waited, my heart galloping. If he didn't answer, *then* what?

But from above me, Bud finally grumbled back, "Keep yer shirt on, will ya?"

I felt boneless with relief as I hustled in the direction of his voice, dodging the glass and fallen boards that littered the floor of the kitchen and the room beyond, which was empty except for a bedraggled staircase against the far wall. I *needed* Bud like you need the feel of solid ground beneath your feet after you've spent too long on a roller coaster.

I reached the foot of the treacherous old stairway and called up, "Bud? Hey, there's a bacon and cheese sandwich with your name on it waiting at some fast-food place down the road! Let's get a move on!"

"Yeah, yeah," he answered. "Come on up, why doncha."

Meanwhile the dog materialized on the landing at the top of the stairs and sat patiently looking down at me with six shining eyes. I pushed fallen ceiling plaster out of the way and slowly climbed, avoiding the ragged holes where the stairs had rotted through. When I finally reached the landing, the dog skittered down the hall and came to a sliding stop outside one of three closed doors that must have been upstairs bedrooms.

And then it, the dog, evaporated into nothingness.

I walked cautiously to the door where it had been and knocked. "Bud? You . . . in there?"

No answer, so I turned the knob and pushed it open a bit. "Hey, Bud?"

He was sitting on a straight chair, looking out the window with his back to me.

I let out my breath in a whoosh that left me light-headed. "Hey, come on, Bud, let's get going! I'm starving, aren't you?"

He didn't turn. In fact, he didn't move at all. "Come over here, will you, son?" he said. "I got something I need to show you right quick."

His voice was so . . . I don't know, tired? Well, of *course* he was tired and so was I. I walked up behind him and bent to look over his shoulder. "What is it, Bud?"

He pointed. "Can you see that small hill yonder a ways, the one with trees?"

I squinted, trying to see what he was talking about. The glass was just too grimy, so I straightened and looked through a place near the top of the window where the glass had gone missing. Beyond the ocean of wheat I saw a series of bumps along the far horizon.

One of the bumps seemed fringed. "I *think* I see the hill with trees."

He nodded. "Our burying place is under those elms. My grandparents, my parents, my little sis. She died of polio while I was in Korea. My Mary is out there as well. My sweet Mary, gone now for ten years."

I said nothing, just thought about how Bud's voice was so *distant*. He sounded like he was in a different room, reading out loud or talking in his sleep.

The wind blew the wheat. Some crows flew by in a tight formation. The scene outside was so peaceful, but it somehow had an edge, a dark border.

"This was your house, then, Bud?" I finally asked. "And we're in . . . Nebraska?"

He nodded. "Lived here with my folks and then for years with my Mary before we had our Janet and moved on to give her more advantages in a bigger place."

I took a step back and looked around the room. There was an old set of iron springs that must once have been part of a bed. Wallpaper hung like loose skin from the walls, too puckered and water-stained for you to tell what color or pattern it might have once been. Wasps' nests were thick in the corners of the ceiling and littered the floor.

"Go along now, boy," Bud said, still without turning. "I'll join you directly."

"I'll just hang out here until you're ready to go, Bud."

"Go on along," he insisted. His voice had a crackle to it when he said that, like a radio transmission sent from far away. I wanted him to face me and to at least explain how we came to be at his old place. But he just kept staring out that filthy window. "Tell her I won't be but a few more minutes," he added weakly.

I shook my head and threw out my arms. "What business is it of *hers*, Bud?" I took a few angry paces across the room and back. "You've done plenty for her already! Now we need to get on the road home and let her hitch a different ride."

He said nothing, so I said, more quietly, "Okay, how about this, Bud. I'll go get the car and bring it closer while you finish getting ready. I think I can drive through the wheat right up to the porch. Okay with that?"

"Yeah, yeah, good plan," he murmured.

On my way out of that sad room I spotted a small patch of

wallpaper that must have been protected for many decades by a dresser or something. I crouched beside it for a few seconds, running my fingers over the pattern—bright blue, yellow, and red wildflowers blooming against a violet sky. So beautiful and eternal, all hope and innocence.

A new wave of anger and frustration rolled through me and I was stumbling over my own feet by the time I made it back down the rotted stairs and through the desolate kitchen. Why did nothing last? What was the point of all that innocent hope in that wallpaper? Who could answer me, huh? *Huh?*

I was shaking all over by the time I got out of the house. I stood on the porch and looked around trying to settle down and breathe right. No sign of the dog. The car looked like a toy some child had lost in the blowing wheat.

I had to get a grip, and I knew a run through sun and wind would help more than anything. Just hiking up the hill to the house had been excruciating, though. My legs were tight and hurt worse than ever today. There was nothing mental I could do to block this much pain, so I gritted my teeth and launched myself down the porch stairs and into the wheat, moving at a pace that was faster than I could have forced myself to move without the downhill slope bouncing me painfully and help-lessly along.

I was halfway back to the car when I remembered that the weird hitchhiker girl had stolen the keys! But how hard could it be to grab her pack, fish them out, and pocket them again? I just hoped I could locate her in all this wheat.

That proved to be easy. She'd returned to her circle of flattened wheat, not far from the Olds. She was lying on her back with her lumpy green pack beneath her head like a pillow and the ankle of one cowboy boot casually jiggling on the opposite bare knee. She was thumbing through a magazine and chewing a wad of gum. Three or four more of those magazines were scattered around her, their pages rippling in the wind.

She rolled to her side when she heard me charge up, propping her head with her hand.

"How do you like my hair, Tucker Graysten?" she called out cheerfully. "No, wait, wait! Don't answer yet!" She sat up and scratched her flaming pink hair into random spikes. "There, *now* you can answer."

All my anger at her finally boiled over. "Do you think this whole thing is a *joke*?" I yelled against the wind. "Okay, so you somehow learned a lethal type of hypnosis, hooray for you. And you go around reading people's minds without any respect for their privacy, and drive them to places they never wanted to go, and then you steal their keys, and then you . . . you have the nerve to ask for an opinion about *hair* choices?"

She knit her brows, looking truly confused. "No," she said, simply. "Only a joke is a joke." She held up her magazine and turned it toward me. "Look at this, Tucker, chocolate cake with chocolate fudge icing! Have you ever heard of chocolate cake?"

I gawked at her for a few seconds. "Everybody's heard of chocolate cake," I muttered, rubbing my face with my hands and shaking my head. What was the use? My anger drained—why cling to it? She was just a total airhead. Hating her was impossible and useless. It would have been like hating a tree, or a shoe.

She began carefully tearing the cake picture from her magazine.

"Oh, come closer and *look*, Tucker!" She held the picture up so I could see. "On the back there's a photo of that airplane that crashed last month! You can even see the teensy people inside!"

She turned the airplane photo toward me and my blood went cold. Those magazines scattered around her makeshift lounge were *my* magazines from the school library!

I dropped to a crouch, laced my fingers behind my neck, and stared straight down at the ground so I could pretend for a few minutes that she didn't exist. I could hear the swish of her gathering those magazines into a stack, though. Then she cleared her throat like someone giving an important speech and began reading the covers out loud.

"*Time Magazine,* October 22, PROPERTY OF CLEVESDALE HIGH SCHOOL, CLEVESDALE, OKLAHOMA," she announced. "*Newsweek* magazine and here in the bottom corner it's stamped PROPERTY OF CLEVESDALE HIGH SCHOOL, CLEVESDALE, OKLAHOMA. This one is *Smithsonian* and it's for the month of September and it's stamped PROPERTY OF CLEVESDALE HIGH SCHOOL, CLEVESDALE, OKLAHOMA. *National Geographic* and up in the corner, kind of light like the library's stamp needs inking, is PROPERTY OF CLEVESDALE HIGH SCHOOL, CLEVESDALE, OKLAHOMA. And the one that had the yummy cake picture, *American Life,* PROPERTY OF CLEVESDALE HIGH SCHOOL, CLEVESDALE, OKLAHOMA."

When she was through, I raised my head and stared at her,

hoping I could send anger her way that would melt her or some-thing. She merely leaned closer to me, wide-eyed.

"So, did you *steal* all these magazines from your school li-brary, Tucker Graysten?"

"Shouldn't that question be did *you* steal them from my *backpack*?" I spat out.

"Guilty!" She held up her hands, laughing. "You caught me red-handed!"

Her palms oozed and dripped with something thick, shiny, and very, very red.

I felt things getting black around the edges so I panted, try-ing to get more air.

"What's the matter, Tuck?" She turned her wrists to look at her palms, then wrinkled her nose. "Ick, I see what you mean. Is this *blood* on my hands?"

She laughed that crazy laugh again and turned her palms back toward me. Now they were just the dry hot pink of her hair dye.

"That wasn't funny." That came out in a whimper. I tried again. "That. Wasn't—"

"It was a cool trick, though, wasn't it?" she interrupted. "Caught red-handed, get it?"

"Why can't you just express your opinions like a normal per-son?" I moaned. "Why do you always have to act like a—"

"Street magician? Tucker Graysten, tell me the honest truth, do you think if I went to a big city, say, Chicago, that I could make a living as a street magician?"

I looked down at the ground again and pushed out, under

my breath, "If you think I have blood on my hands, why can't you just . . . *say* so."

At first she said nothing. I assumed she hadn't heard me. It would have been almost impossible for her to have heard me. But then she asked, "Why would I think *that*?"

I jumped to my feet, took a couple of angry and painful strides toward her, and yelled, "Because I bailed out of the Mustang before that wicked curve, of course! You *know* that from invading my memories. You're accusing me of *abandoning* my best friends!"

She sighed. "Tucker Graysten, everything in this world is not about *you*, you know. I was just practicing a new trick with that blood-on-my-hands thing. And also for your information, I am *not* in the business of judging people, thank you very much. My job is hard enough without my having to be some kind of judge or jury or . . . or *dictator* or something in my spare time, of which I don't even *have* any!"

The idea of this weird girl holding down a job was outrageous. And hadn't she said earlier that she and the dog were, what . . . co-workers? That proved it. She was a psycho, just totally nuts. I had to remember that and not let her get to me like she'd been doing.

I sat down in the wheat, pulled up my legs, and planted my elbows on my knees. "So, okay, where do you work?" I asked with a weary snort. "A fast-food restaurant?"

"I'm a laborer," she said. "See my calluses?" She held her

hands toward me again, palms out in a butterfly shape. "I get blisters you wouldn't believe, Tucker Graysten."

Her palms were a mess, all right. All oozing blisters and leathery gray calluses, just like she'd described. But then again, after witnessing that last trick, I had to assume she could make her hands be just about any way she wanted them to be.

"That's why I asked you if you thought I could be a street performer," she said in a wistful way. "I'm always dreaming of a different job, though even if I found something, I don't know if I could quit the job I've got. I mean, I've had it like forever and ever."

"You can quit any job," I muttered, not because I knew what I was talking about but because I was exhausted and it's what people *always* said. "If your job sucks, just quit."

"You don't know my boss." She shivered and stood. "Here, I'm done with these."

She threw the stack of magazines toward me, and they spread their pages and flew in slow motion like five gaudy parrots. They stopped in midair and fell straight to the ground in front of me as though some invisible hunter had shot them through their hearts.

I stared, openmouthed, at where they formed a quivering line between me and the crazy hitchhiker. Each magazine had fallen open to the picture I stole it for.

She stood up and strolled over to squat beside the *American Life*. She tucked the cake picture back into it and I watched the rip where she'd torn it out close like a sutured wound. Then the cake page turned all on its own to reveal that falling airplane.

"A plane falling from the sky," she whispered. "You wanted to see the expressions on those faces, didn't you, Tucker Graysten? *That's* what fascinated you. Don't you think I know why you collected these pictures? Death is the last frontier, and you think you can learn its terrain, its language, and its customs without ever leaving your cozy home."

When I felt her breath on my neck, I realized she had somehow moved to stand right behind me. In fact, suddenly she was looking at those pictures from over my shoulder.

She smelled like . . . what *was* that smell? Plants? No, she smelled like dirt.

XII

THE WIND CAME UP and rustled all five magazines closed.

"There's a surer way to learn what you want to know, Tucker Graysten," she breathed into my ear. "Give me what you have in your right back pocket and presto, you'll know."

She snaked one of her hands under my arm. It loomed there in front of me, cobra-like, asking for something, needing me to feed it with something, a callused and creased hand so very old, ancient even, thin and in fact almost . . . skeletal.

My ears rang as I scrambled sideways like a crab, getting away from her.

"You don't even *know* what I've got in my right back pocket!" I crouched there, shaking all over, my hands shielding my face on each side so that I wouldn't make the mistake of turning and looking directly at those spiral eyes of hers. "And even if you did know, why would you even *want* it?"

"How many times do I have to tell you? It's mine, *that's* why I want it!"

I shook my head, fast and hard. "No, you're wrong. A teacher gave it to me just . . . yesterday. It's only an old coin she had, sort of a good luck charm, of no value at all beyond that."

The wind began to spiral. The magazines were taken up into that dark spin and carried far off toward the vanishing point of the horizon. I watched the bright shreds of them being spit into the sky in all directions.

She stepped in front of where I huddled. The last thing I wanted was to look up at her, but my will wasn't strong enough to resist her. It ached, like the rest of me.

"Tucker Graysten?" she said quietly. "My coin, if you please?"

I braced myself and shook my head, trying frantically to remember what Mrs. Beetlebaum had said about that coin, that obolus. You put one in the mouth of the newly dead, wasn't that it? It was the fare to the underworld, the payment you had to make to the guy who rowed the boat from the land of the living to the land of the dead.

I opened my eyes to a slit and carefully looked at her, expecting anything.

She was just herself. "Oh, fine, then." She sulked, twirling a spike of hair around one finger. "If you're too selfish to part with that worthless coin, then let's get back to playing our game. *Trade* me something for this green Bic. . . ." She stopped, frowning.

I gave a quick, hysterical laugh. "You haven't got the lighter now, remember?"

She rolled her eyes. "Cherry Berry likes you," she grumbled. She stomped to her pack and began rooting around in it. "And

for your information, I've got too much work to do to be playing stupid games anyhow, Tucker Graysten."

She maneuvered a huge notebook from the overstuffed
pack's murky depths, and I caught enough of a look at it to
know it was one of those silly razzle-dazzle three-ring shiny
deals you can buy at any discount store. It had a bright lime
green cover labeled *Dream Journal* in elaborate glitter script.
There was a unicorn sticker in the corner and in the center was
a holographic picture of some female movie star or singer, some
dark-haired diva that I couldn't identify and wasn't the least bit
interested in anyhow.

She unclipped a pen from the spiral and went to sit on the
ground beside Bud's car, leaning back against a fender. "I gotta
record this pickup," she called to me in a pouty voice, flipping
impatiently through the pages. "My boss'll have a *fit* if I forget."

She found the page she wanted, took the pen from her teeth,
and bent to work.

Her pack was a bit closer to me than to her. I sidled over to it
as quickly and quietly as I could, then sank to my knees beside
it. A glance told me she was wrapped up in whatever it was she
was doing, so I began moving her messy stuff around, searching for the car keys. A baseball-sized knot of grape bubble gum
wrappers was one of many things clogging my view. I pushed
the sticky mess aside and heard a sharp hiss.

A small snake looked angrily up at me from its gum-paper
nest, rattling its tail.

I jumped to my feet and hustled backward. My hands were

shaking, so I stuck them under my armpits and tried to act calm. "Do you . . . do you know you have a . . ."

"There." She closed her notebook with a satisfied nod and looked over at me. "Since there are 701,843 trails in the world, it takes a while to find the right one. Once I find it, all I have to do is put a checkmark beside it, but first I have to find it and that takes—"

I couldn't bring myself to pretend interest in her imaginary job. "Do you know that you . . . you have a baby rattlesnake living in the grunge at the bottom of your pack?"

"Actually, it's a fully grown pygmy rattler." She stood, stretched, then slipped her pen back into the spiral of her tacky Kmart notebook. She sashayed toward me, her notebook against her chest and her arms crossed over it. "I'm thinking about collecting pygmy rattlers. To be honest, Tucker Graysten, even though I know you love my hair this color, I would absolutely *adore* having hair like *hers*."

She shoved the notebook under my nose and pointed to the diva on the front.

She was one of those Greek goddesses, the really, really nasty one with snakes for hair who could turn people to stone with her fierce ugliness. And this picture wasn't just a hologram, either. The goddess was actually moving, or at least the snakes growing from her head were moving, writhing and hissing, spitting and coiling. . . .

"Medusa just has the best hair ever," the hitchhiker girl breathed, stepping even closer to me so she was right beneath my chin, mere inches away. "Do you think I might be able to get hair implants or something? I mean, if I had the snakes?"

My head was filling with her smell of cold dirt and grape bubble gum. I could feel an icy chill coming off her, right through her thick motorcycle jacket. She was nuts, just nuts, coiled to strike just like that pet snake of hers was coiled in its gum wrapper nest, and I would *not* look directly at her spiral eyes again no matter what.

"Nobody could—could know exactly how many trails there are in the world," I stammered, buying time. Bud would surely get out here any minute and *he* would get her to hand over the keys. Nobody played games with Bud. "And even if you did have some weird job of recording trails, you couldn't record 701,843 of *anything* in that cheap little notebook of yours."

She drew in a hurt breath and her hand went to her mouth. "Cheap?" she whispered.

"You might as well back off," I told her quietly. "Nothing you say, nothing you do is going to make me look you in the eye again."

For a while, she said nothing. She even backed away from me a couple of steps. I could think a little better as that wicked dirt-grape smell emptied from my head.

"Okay, I'm sorry for being such a know-it-all, Tucker," she finally said, her voice small and humble.

Out the corner of my right eye, I could see her tapping the toe of one boot, then scuffing it back and forth in a way that might possibly be apologetic.

"I was just showing off when I told you there were exactly 701,843 trails. That was silly. Of *course* no one can know how many trails there are at any one second. Not when new ones come into existence all the time."

I shrugged, keeping my eyes glued to my own feet as I turned my back to her. "I'm going to the house to try to get Bud to hustle," I said gruffly. "Why don't you give me back the car keys so I can drive up and he doesn't have to walk so far?"

"There are trails over land, but also under every ocean," she continued as though I hadn't spoken. "And there are trails right through the air, like the one the Mustang blazed when it sailed off that bluff like a great red flying fish. A sweet trail, that one, fun while it lasted. Your friends thought so. They were laughing. Or . . . I could be wrong. Maybe they were actually . . . screaming?"

My heart slammed, hard, and I felt dizzy with grief and anger. I wheeled back around and focused all that hot emotion on her smug face, wishing I could melt her.

She shrugged, innocent as a statue. "Bud's dying, you know," she said in a small, little-girl voice, shifting her weight from foot to foot. "I give him twenty-nine minutes, thirty-two seconds, using your human measurements. And when he dies, that'll be that, you'll stay or I'll take you. But if you stay with that poison splinter still embedded, I guarantee you'll be putting out another call to me, pronto. And the next time, I won't be so nice. It'll just be 'Get into the boat and give me the money. Too bad you didn't tell yourself what you needed to know when I gave you a chance the *first* time, buster.'"

"Tell *me* what *I* need to know?" I shook my head. "You're crazy! None of what you're saying makes sense! Bud's tough. He'll probably outlive us all. And anyhow, nobody jokes about an old person's death. That's just . . . tasteless and cruel!"

"What're we doing here anyhow, Tucker Graysten?" she asked, this time sadly shaking her head. "You called me with your infected legs and your game of squatting by the TV to see what you'd look like without a head and your horrific magazine picture collection and the threats you made to an innocent ant that was walking up your window *and* your out-of-control driving. This is not to mention the paranoid fantasy you've taken up where your best friend visits your dreams with sarcastic comments. So just man up and yank that teensy splinter of nasty truth from your heart so we can see if you bleed out from it. There's a teensy chance you *may* actually live, so don't you think it's worth the effort? If you find out you *can't* live with it, you save me the trouble of a return trip by taking a seat with Bud and me when we hit the road in twenty-eight minutes and five seconds, using your human measurements. And *I* collect the coin, of course. And in answer to what you were thinking before, no, I can't take it, *you* have to hand it over."

She rubbed her fingers together greedily, and for just the space of an eyeblink, she turned into something ancient and withered. I let out a sharp burst of sound, maybe it was a scream, and backed farther away from her.

She laughed and crossed her arms. "When I was fairly new to this job, I had a pickup I've never forgotten. Old guy, weird name. Socrates. Most people have a few little things to say on the trip, but boy, this guy was a *talker*. Gab, gab, gab. I forget most of it, but this one thing has stuck in my head all these years. 'The unexamined life is not worth living.' You got the idea he'd said that before to various audiences, and of course he was exaggerating for effect. Still, it's something to think about, right, Tucker Graysten? To me, and this is my professional take on things, to *me* it seems pretty likely that the unexamined life will slip right through your fingers."

She gave her thumbnail a chew, then wiped it on her skirt.

"Take druggies, for instance. Usually they're asleep when I come—in a coma, that is. They keep telling me that same thing *you* keep telling me, that they didn't give me a pickup call. Still, they *did*, right? By opening that prescription bottle or snorting that line or filling that syringe? Whoa, those are some of the loudest calls I get! I mean, the instant you hear any of those things, you're on standby to roll! I'm just saying. Bud's dying, so *you've* got twenty-seven minutes and twelve seconds left to do some deeper examining. That is, according to your human measurement. To me, it's maybe half a second."

Her weirdness was enough to break your mind, but something even weirder had started to happen to the landscape right behind her. The sky had almost instantly gone from being cloudless and blue to being a leaden shade of dark purple, with lightning clawing through it like skeletal hands. Then over her shoulder I watched in horror as a huge, green wedge came barreling toward us through the wheat, cutting a swath that must have been a couple of city blocks wide. Within mere seconds it had moved from the distant horizon to so close to us that the roar of its approach drowned out what the weird hitchhiker girl was saying.

"It's a *flash flood*!" I yelled, my voice a shriek of disbelief. "Quick, give me the keys! If the car gets submerged, we'll never get it started again!"

She flopped a hand, dismissing my worries. "Nah, the car'll be fine," she yelled back. "Trail number 11,404 does this all the time. There was a river right where we're standing a century and a half ago, but over the decades it changed course. When your dimension and ours overlap, trail number 11,404 sometimes comes unhinged in time. I mean, it gets unpredictable, sometimes wet like it was in 1850, sometimes dry enough to build a house on like it was in 1910 when Bud's parents built this one. This river, the one that once flowed here and is back for a visit, was actually a point of no return on trail number 11,404, better known to you mortals as the Oregon Trail. Interesting, huh, Tucker Graysten? Once you got a wagon filled with heavy stuff across it, you would *so* not want to change your mind and go back."

"Back?" My ears were ringing.

She rolled her eyes. "Back *home*, silly. Everybody on every trail comes from home. They're going everywhere, but they all start from the same place. Home."

While she'd been chatting, the water had swept through

where we were standing. It was up to the top pockets of her motorcycle jacket. With a little grunt, she hefted her pack up onto her head and used both hands to balance it teetering there.

I felt the cold murk reach my own waist and I stuck a protective hand into the water and over my back jeans pocket, the one holding Mrs. Beetlebaum's coin. *Tucker, put it in your pocket and keep it there!* The weirder this got, the more I wished I'd asked Mrs. B. more questions, or listened harder, or something.

I cupped my mouth with the other hand and swiveled as far as I could to yell toward the house, "Bud, put on some *speed*! There's been a flood and the water is rising fast! We gotta get out of here right *now*!"

When I looked back at her, the crazy hitchhiker was squinting into space, her eyes dreamy. "Tucker Graysten, can you describe to me the taste of chocolate cake with chocolate icing?"

I splashed a wave at her, hoping a cold, watery slap in the face would focus her attention. "We're about to drown here!" I yelled at the top of my lungs. "We need a plan, not your spaced-out raving about things coming unhinged in time!"

For once, she looked alarmed. In fact, she turned a lighter shade of pale. "Did I say that? That is *so* classified. Please, please forget I mentioned it, okay?"

I tried, unsuccessfully, to pull one boot up from the mud. "We could *die* here, can't you see that? If we're not out of here in the next few minutes, I'd say we're cooked!"

She shrugged. "People die everywhere," she said.

And with that, her voice somehow became the wind. Not

the howling wind that had moved the wheat and not the restless wind that now whistled over the river, but a mysterious breeze that rattled like the dry cedar needles on the gnarled trees in the Clevesdale Cemetery where Trey, and Steve, and Zero had been buried for almost two complete days now.

People die everywhere. Those three lonely words and the forlorn way she'd said them suddenly made me tired to the bone, so tired that my weariness felt like sweet relief. What was the point of this struggle, this tug-of-war with her and the wind and water?

What difference did anything make, really?

What difference did even drowning make, really?

I lifted my eyes, and she met them with those eyes of hers that were often dizzying spirals. But this time, they were soft green pools of welcoming liquid shade.

"When your call came into headquarters, Tucker, my boss happened to take it," she whispered, sounding very near, nearer than she was. "He told me it was a double pickup, right at the edge of Kansas City, the beginning point of trail number 11,404, better known to you mortals as the Oregon Trail. Surprise, surprise, Tucker Graysten. We've been on the Oregon Trail this whole time, from K. C. to here in Nebraska! Bud, well, I immediately understood his call. He was ready. His time was here and he knew it. Your call, though, was something else. You're young, no lethal habits. I could see when I read you that you care about your family, you care about your friends. And then it hit me—because you've had so much practice not telling people what you think, you were able to hide your thinking even from yourself when something happened that you couldn't stand to know. Listen, that kind of thing always festers and when it *does* . . ." She drew one index finger across her throat.

I felt myself circling down through an endless blue tunnel, as though I'd been sucked right into her eyes. "Trey said I could be our designated driver," I heard myself croak.

"Yessss!" she hissed. "See? You *did* know where that missing sliver of truth was hiding in your story. But you've merely exposed it. You've *still* got to pull it from your heart so you can look at it directly and decide if it'll kill you. It's not only that you can't drive a car in this condition, it's that you can't drive your own *life* in this condition. So really, what've you got to lose?"

I'd never cried in my life, but I came close then. "I'm too . . . tired," I pushed out.

Young Tucker, you innocent wonder, you can be our designated driver tonight!

I was the slimiest creature in that entire muddy river. I felt hooked, harpooned. Harpooned right through the heart by a massive weapon, struggling in the water, a thing too disgusting to struggle but struggling still, just out of habit.

I needed an escape route. Not from the water, but from myself.

"Guilt is unbreathable," she whispered, and her windy voice came drifting raggedly across the water. "Guilt is what's killing you, Tucker Graysten. You've been drowning in it since the moment you saw that burning Mustang."

I moved my arm slowly against the strong current and stuck

three fingers inside the sodden denim of my back pocket. I felt the rough edge of the coin Mrs. Beetlebaum had given me. I didn't know how it worked or why it worked, but I was suddenly sure it was the portal out of myself.

I extended my arm, my closed fist. "What you want is in my hand."

Her mouth dropped open and her eyes glittered. "Hold on!" she called, and she tossed her pack lightly across several feet of water and onto the top of Bud's car. An instant later she just sort of *leaped* out of the water herself and was suddenly sitting on her pack in the center of the green oval island that was all that was left of the Olds.

She leaned far forward, stretching both hands toward me and wiggling her fingers like a kid reaching for candy. "Toss it to me now, Tucker Graysten!"

I raised my arm, but as I pulled back for a good pitch, somewhere behind me I heard glass breaking, then Bud bellowed, "Hey, kid, don't give her *nothin',* you hear?"

I saw her eyes shift from soft, green inviting pools to dark and luminous stones as she jerked her head up and looked past me, at the house. My muscles went weak and wobbly. Something like an electric current had been pouring through me from her eyes, and it'd suddenly been switched off when she'd shifted her attention.

I shook my head, trying to clear my wits, and felt water lapping at my chin. I was up to my neck and the river was still rising.

I tried to turn toward Bud's voice, but my legs were sunk too deep in the mud. I lost my balance and gulped brackish water, but on my second try I saw the old house with my peripheral vision. The river was lapping at the porch, but Bud was leaning out the upstairs bedroom window where he'd been before. It was outlined in jagged glass, and he held one shoe like a hammer in his blunt-fingered hand.

"Don't listen to that fairy girl, kid!" he bellowed. "Stick that coin back in your pocket and park it there for another fifty, sixty years! Seventy, even!"

"Look at *me*, Tucker Graysten!" the crazy hitchhiker girl screeched.

I snapped my head back around to face her. For a fraction of a second I glimpsed something dark and shaggy crouched atop the Olds. It gave off a rank wind that stirred the water into small and angry waves. Then, in the space of an eyeblink, it was gone, the water flowed along quickly but normally again, and the crazy hitchhiker girl had taken the place of that *thing* on the almost-submerged roof of the car. She was sitting on the edge now, kicking both boots through the water and scratching her hair energetically with both hands. Her brows were knit in an expression of, what? Indecision? Hard thought?

Bud yelled, "Leave off on the kid, can't you? You done it before, remember? There on that battlefield in Korea? My buddies all in pieces and me the only survivor in that trench slick with blood? I wanted to go with them, I begged you even, but it wasn't my time. So why can't you give this kid the same break?

He's confused! He's even younger and greener than *I* was, and let me tell you, I was *plenty* confused."

Her eyes bugged with frustration and she threw up her arms. "I've tried to give him a break, Bud, but it's *complicated*! I'm not perfect, I *admit* it, okay? Bud, *you* didn't have an obolus to tempt me! Hardly anyone has them these days, so *I* hardly ever get *paid*!"

There was a sudden frantic splashing and the dog bobbed up from nowhere, just appeared from under the water! He swam to the Olds and pulled himself up onto the roof with a great scratching commotion, then he began shiver-shaking himself.

She groaned. "*Just* what I need! Cherry Berry, why didn't you go *home* like I *told* you to?" She shielded her face with an upraised hand and leaned away from the mess. "You don't *belong* in this dimension, and you *smell* like wet dog!"

The dog sank down with two of its chins on its paws and the other one in her lap. She shook her head but automatically began scratching his ears. After a few seconds she got that calm look on her face that people get when they're scratching the head of a dog.

"Oh, Tucker," she murmured, "Bud's got a point. I'm not some sort of monster. Like I told you, I'm just a simple laborer, and money means a lot to me. With enough coins, I can maybe retire and try for that street magician gig? But they quit making those coins hundreds of years ago, so there aren't that many around. The thing is, I can practically *feel* that obolus of yours in my hand, so tantalizing. But like Bud said, I *do* cut deals with kids like you sometimes, especially when they're as innocent as Bud was, there in that trench in Korea. It turned out he'd issued a pickup call mostly from sheer panic, partly from grief, also partly from shock and pain. When he'd told himself his story, we both knew he wanted desperately to live."

She narrowed her eyes and focused them on me. "*You* aren't that innocent, though."

I felt that electric current sizzle through my brain and into my arms and legs again.

"Bud and I have to hit the road," she said as thunder boomed. "It's now or never, Tucker Graysten. Pull that splinter of truth from your heart and take a good look at yourself. You can't drive because . . ."

Her eyes narrowed to laser beams. I felt them cutting and cutting, going soul deep into me through all the layers of lies and justifications and outright denials I'd wrapped around the fragile truth as I'd tried my dead-level best to hide it from myself.

". . . I flunked my designated driver's test." It slid from me in a whisper, but she was right—it *felt* like I'd yanked a huge, rough splinter from my heart. I screamed a long, gut-wrenching scream, and at the end of it I couldn't move.

I felt paralyzed in every muscle, rigid as a stick or a small log, snagged in the bottomless mud. I couldn't think, or talk, or figure out how to breathe the watery air.

XIII

I WAS DROWNING. At first I couldn't make my brain take that in, but when my lungs began to burn, things got real in a hurry—I was *drowning*! I was stuck to my knees in mud, and I could tell by the clammy pressure against my ears and the skin of my face that the rising water had finally covered all of me but the very top of my head. I felt the air leaving a farewell fingerprint the size of a quarter on my scalp, and I knew with great, sad clarity that I wouldn't be feeling the air against my skin or anything else much longer because I had just taken my first deep breath of cold water.

Bright pain hit my bronchial tubes, then eased as my mind began going numb. I saw my arms floating up, and I began to fall slowly backward into the arms of the river.

The last breath I would ever take was leaking from me in a fountain of bubbles when something big plummeted into the water, scattering those tiny globes of air and churning everything to mud. I felt jolted in three places as the dog grabbed me by the denim behind my left knee, by one belt loop of my jeans, and by my left ear, which it held gently inside its right set of teeth. We flew straight upward from the water.

I came around enough to look down, where I saw a small whirlpool that marked where I'd been trapped until a second or two before. It happened *so* fast, in an instant, and with my ear immobilized in the dog's jaws, I couldn't turn my head to see more details. All I know is limp parts of me were hanging from each of its mouths like scraps of clothing it had pulled from someone's laundry line.

I was dropped onto my side on top of Bud's car, where I drew up my knees and began coughing my guts out. I sucked in about as much water as I coughed back out until I finally realized the entire roof of the car was submerged a couple of inches. I rolled painfully onto my back and stared up at the purple, stormy sky, trying to get my muscles to quit spasming, retching up muddy water and saliva and a bit of blood. Each time I grabbed a breath, the tangy smell of dog spit hit me and cleared my head for a second.

I finally forced myself to sit up. Where *was* everybody? The house was still mostly above-water, but it looked like there could be a foot or so of flooding downstairs. If Bud was still inside, he might be trapped by that much water. Where were the hitch-hiker girl and the dog? I closed my eyes and slumped there, my elbows on my knees, trying to get my brain to work well enough to make a plan for getting to Bud.

I eventually noticed that my right hand was still clenched tight around Mrs. Beetlebaum's coin. I used my left hand to peel back my fingers. When the coin was exposed to the air, steam came off it. Or maybe it was smoke because right after I twisted to the side and eased the obolus back into my rear pocket, I felt a sharp stab of pain and watched an angry blister the size and shape of that coin rising on my palm.

While I was staring at my hand, I heard a quick swishing sound, like the last ounce or so of bathwater going down a drain. I looked up and the floodwater was gone, every drop of it. There was just the old house with its shattered window on a rise of bright wheat and me on the hot roof of Bud's car. The dry stalks of grain whispered hoarsely as the wind rocketed through them. An autumn sun beat down on things with all its might.

I sank to my back again with my arms spread wide, letting the sunshine into every molecule of me. I'd nearly drowned, so I knew I wanted to live, and I hated myself for wanting that since I couldn't imagine living my life now, knowing what I'd done. But there it was, the cowardly truth. I didn't want to die.

I folded my arms across my face and lay there groaning and rocking side to side.

"Come on down here, boy. I got a couple things to tell you right quick."

"Bud!" I flipped to my stomach and hung my head over the edge of the roof. He was in the driver's seat with his hands on the wheel, right where he belonged.

"Come on down, son," he repeated, still gazing straight ahead.

I swung through the open passenger window and dropped into the seat beside him. My legs throbbed in a new way that made my stomach turn, like they were filled with something toxic that was rising to fill the rest of me. "Bud, let's get *outta* here, *now!*"

He didn't seem to hear me. "I want to be sure you can still locate the small hill from this vantage, the one with trees I spoke to you about earlier."

I was too jittery and sick to sit still for this. "Sure I can, Bud. Now let's *go!*"

"Good." He just sat there, gripping the wheel.

Should I try to get him to trade seats with me? *Could* I drive, even if he'd let me? Bud and I had both flunked driver's tests, and the one I'd flunked was so much worse. I held on to my own arms to keep from shaking apart.

"All right, so I've told you where the cemetery's at, and the other thing I got to tell you is to change the oil real often with a big car like this. Now listen, I'd never let her go past three thousand miles. And there are tools in the trunk. Don't be tempted to take them out and use them for whatnot around the house. Keep them there in the trunk so when the need arises, they'll be handy."

Then Bud suddenly turned to face me for the first time and I nearly jumped from the car. His *eyes* were wrong. They were too . . . I want to say flat, but that's not exactly right. The light in them had gone out, that was it. They seemed made of glass.

"The little fairy girl was kneeling beside Tommy when daylight finally reached into that trench in Korea," he said in a precise whisper, as though giving me a play-by-play of something he was just now watching. "Then presently, she stood and whistled through her teeth, one long, sharp whistle. And that fine roan horse Tommy had back home in Nebraska came galloping right toward us across that battlefield. I saw its legs pass through at least a dozen dead boys as easily as a hot knife passes through butter."

Bud turned from me to stare into the distance at his family cemetery. "I believe she provides folks with their most fondly remembered transport when she takes them."

"Buh—Bud?" I stammered. "By . . . by fairy girl, you mean . . . you mean ferry girl, right? Like she . . . ferries people across . . . across the Acheron to the . . . land of the dead?"

"Yeah, that's right," he answered in an offhand way, like I'd asked if he used ketchup with his fries. "So I heard an engine shortly after the mortar shell hit, and I *thought* I saw a motorcycle fly out of that trench with that poker-playing city boy Clark Jackson atop it. I figured at the time I was seeing things, hallucinating from my own bad wounds. But now I think different. Notice how we came straight to the Ford truck last night once she joined us in the car? She drove us right to it." He shook his head, smiling. "I sure didn't expect to find my dad's truck still up here at the old homeplace. I admit I had no real idea where it ended up, but I sure am glad to know it was never sold."

What was he talking about? We *hadn't* come straight to the truck. The truck had been a wild-goose chase that ended with the Chiefs game that ended with . . . *her*.

"Bud, you . . . you don't look so good."

He shrugged. "Tommy stood up in that bloody trench, then swung up onto his horse with both his legs like they'd been before the shell hit," he whispered. "And then *she* was somehow up there in front of him, straddling that bareback roan with the reins in her hands. She looked at me over her shoulder, then she joined her eyes to mine in such a fierce way I had no choice but to let her into my head. Sometimes I think we were locked there for hours, me helpless and about to bleed out and her looking down at me from atop that horse, reading my thoughts. Other times I think it surely couldn't have took more than a minute. I was suffering physical pain and I guess what you'd call emotional pain. I remember all that real clear. I wanted to die, living hurt so bad. But while that fairy girl plumbed my mind, I began to think more and more about my Mary back home and how much I needed to see her again. So finally, I shook my head, and the fairy girl turned around forward and flicked the reins. Tommy's roan took off at a gallop and they sailed right away. Next thing I knew, I woke up in the field hospital."

He added, so softly I barely heard, "When we were both young boys, I often rode behind Tommy on that horse, so I reckon she saw a chance to take us tandem and spare herself some effort if I was of a mind to go right then. She got me to understand it wasn't enough to say yeah, yeah, okay, so I wanta live, not with what I'd seen and the wounds I had. No, the deal was if she agreed to leave me there, I had to agree to fight *hard* to live, hard as in any other battle. With all the blood I'd lost and all those soul tattoos, I couldn't have survived for long even in the hospital without a real decision behind it."

Bud suddenly looked worse than exhausted. He looked green-ish around his mouth and eyes. I needed to get food into him immediately, and then I needed to get him home to his La-Z-Boy and his quiet routine. I was sick and soul-tattooed myself, and I longed to be in the deep green grass beside the radishes in the hoop house, where I could try to begin figuring out how to live with myself, or at least how to go through the motions.

"Bud . . . do . . . do you have the keys?"

"No, I imagine *she's* got 'em, but don't worry about it."

I slumped in the seat, shaking my head. One of us would *have* to drive out of there. I'd watched Trey hotwire the Mustang to start it a couple of times, so I dropped to my side and swung my head down beneath the dashboard, hooking my legs over the back of the front seat. I was hanging upside down like that, searching for the right wires, when a mechanical sound started up somewhere outside. The noise was so shockingly man-made after all the hours of only blowing wind and rushing water that I raised my head, banging it hard and opening the cuts from Trey's locker vent.

I swung back upright, wiping away blood with my sleeve. "What's going on, Bud?" I demanded in a whisper. That rhythmic thrum was growing louder and louder, but I couldn't see where it could be coming from. "Bud! What *is* that, do you know?"

"My truck," Bud answered matter-of-factly. "What else would it be, huh?"

He was staring at the back west corner of the house. At first nothing was different over there, but then sure enough, a truck came rumbling from around that corner, so shiny black it strobed against the blue Nebraska sky. It had big round headlights mounted on delicate chrome stems. My mouth fell open.

"Didn't I tell you she was a looker?" Bud asked huskily. "I'm glad to see she's been kept real nice in the shed out back, too."

Any other time, with my head not hammering and my lips less cracked, I would have given a respectful whistle. All those square and shiny black surfaces. The elegantly thin whitewall tires, a tidy spare mounted like an ornament just beneath the left window. The smooth running boards beneath the two doors, like in gangster movies.

The crazy hitchhiker girl was driving. That is, the ferry girl was driving, though she seemed too flimsy to be driving anything, let alone something like this truck. Her bright hair was all of her that was visible above the steering wheel. It looked like a parrot on a curved black perch.

She drove up even with us and braked when her driver's window was maybe ten feet from my passenger window. She let the truck idle there, burping and rattling, as she pushed open the door with her boot. She slid down from the high driver's seat, spread her motorcycle jacket on the running board, and sat on it.

Then she planted her elbows on her bony white knees and smiled at me, holding a crooked yellow cigarette between her middle finger and her thumb.

"Got a light?" she called, shading her eyes with her free

hand. The day had become incredibly clear and bright. The sun was bleaching everything but the deep blue sky and the deep black car to the brown tones of old photos.

I dug Trey's lighter from my pocket. "You're gonna kill yourself with those cancer sticks," I muttered with false swagger, trying not to show her how sick and weak I was. I'd yanked that splinter of poison truth from my heart, and like she'd warned, I'd nearly bled out. I hadn't died, but if she knew how miserable I felt, how filled with self-disgust and hopelessness, she might decide I was close enough.

"It's a roll-your-own like they smoked in the 1930s. I found it smashed in the seat of this truck. You could lose a small cat in the padding of these seats."

I glanced over at Bud, who still sat motionless behind the steering wheel of the Olds, staring straight ahead. Quietly, I opened my door and shuffled painfully across to the truck. My hands weren't all that steady as I flicked the lighter, but it lit.

I held the flame down to her.

"Cigs won't kill me," she said when she'd lit up. "Nothing will kill me. But I'm not allowed to eat on the job. I get to smoke and chew gum, but I don't get to eat. And since I work every second of every single day that means no chocolate cake, ever. Not even half of a banana Popsicle. Not. Ever. Not once in eternity."

She took a deep drag, then breathed out a large, smoky sigh of regret over all that forbidden dessert. I noticed her eyeing my pockets, looking again for the obolus.

"You're greedy, you know," I heard myself say, covering that pocket with my hand.

"Yeah," she agreed with a shrug. "I'm greedy, you're greedy, everybody's greedy for something. I'm greedy for passengers because once in a rare while they pay me and I like money. With enough money I can maybe retire in a few thousand more years and become a street magician and eat cake to my heart's content. You're greedy for . . . what *are* you greedy for, Tucker Graysten? I told *you,* now *you* have to tell *me.*"

She changed, became sharper-edged so that her face looked snake-like, all scales and bones. I thought I even saw the pupils of her eyes stretch upward to become vertical as she added, in something like a hiss, "Tucker Graysten, what are you greedy for? *Say* it!"

"I'm greedy for . . . for life." I thought my chest would implode with pure, raw shame.

She smiled and nodded and relaxed back against the truck door. "You look really horrible, worse even than when I first put eyes on you three minutes ago, my time. But your eyes then were frantic, and now they're sad. No, you're not anywhere *near* ready to go where *we're* going, Tucker. You just want to go home, where all the trails begin."

"But it's not fair for me to . . ."

That's as far as I could get. There was a lump in my throat I couldn't push past.

". . . to crave life so much when Trey is dead? And Steve and

Zero are dead as well? No, it's not fair, you're right. You *were* their designated driver, after all."

She took another long drag on that home-rolled cigarette. Then she noticed a tiny bug bite on her knee and bent to give that all her attention.

"Remember when Janet said she didn't want to take chances with you?" she murmured, scratching. "But *you* said to yourself that all the chances had already been taken?" She spit on her finger and rubbed that spit into the bite. "Boy, were you wrong."

She jerked her head up and snapped her fingers and I instantly began seeing a homemade movie flickering against the shiny door of Bud's old truck. It turned out to feature quick little everyday snippets of my life. Me learning to walk, climbing a tree, going off the high dive at the pool, riding the Tilt-A-Whirl in fourth grade four times in a row until I was too dizzy to stand, kissing Jerilyn Brookner in fifth grade, punching Trey when he stole my pocketknife, touching my tongue to a frozen mailbox, buying a crossbow, breaking my arm, breaking my other arm, going out for soccer, getting punched by Trey for losing his harmonica, hugging my dad before I went to bed on the last night I saw him . . .

She snapped her fingers again and the movie vaporized, taking the wind out of me along with it. I bent with my hands on my knees, disoriented and breathless, panting like I'd panted the night I'd been running along the bluff road and had come upon the nightmare sight of those broken white guardrails, those thick knotted wires still bobbing in the hot wind of the Mustang's recent passing on its way to fiery oblivion. . . .

"Just a small sample, Tucker. About one-tenth of a percentage of the big chances you took before the age of thirteen. There are new chances every day. Quit taking them and you start sending out a signal for me to pick you up. There are a thousand things to make you stop taking chances and only one reason not to stop, that reason being life. So. You flunked your designated driver's test. It was a big deal. Now you've smartened up and you'll take the test again. You'll only have to take it every time you get behind the wheel, that's somewhere around seventy thousand to two hundred thousand more times." She sighed. "Do you think spit works on bug bites? I heard it did, but I'm beginning to doubt it."

I sucked in air and asked, weakly, hoping my question wouldn't trigger a great reveal by the shaggy thing I'd glimpsed three or four times today, "If you're Charon, why aren't you a dark-haired ugly old guy with a beard and a Greek toga?"

She shrugged, still scratching. "That's how the Greeks saw me, at least the guys who hung around in the Agora writing plays and telling stories while their poor wives stayed home and did the drudge work. They figured I'd look like them—male, bearded, solemn, only not as golden and handsome as they saw themselves and those so-called heroes they were so dazzled by. But let me tell you something, those 'heroes' they liked to go on and on about were basically a bunch of spoiled little boys with too much leisure time on their hands. That Achilles, for instance, always picking fights, never letting anyone else have a fair turn in any sporting competition."

She rolled her eyes. "I decided to experiment with fashion because of *them*, frankly. Why should I stay dull and ugly and male all the time just because dull, ugly males imagined me like themselves, only duller and uglier? I can change the look, the voice, even the attitude. It just takes a second. I mean, I'm a good mimic, granted. But the difficult thing is *actual* fashion. Creating your own unique self. Only humans can decide who and what they're going to be or *if* they're going to be."

"You're supposed to have a *boat*," I told her.

I was thinking about Zero's uncle's boat and how glad I'd been to have it match the illustration in Mrs. B.'s book. When I tried to picture my friends crossing that mysterious, fog-shrouded dark water, I needed every bit of comfort I could get.

"I keep my boat anchored at the river Acheron. There used to be a full-time guy that brought passengers to me, his name was Hermes? Well, the boss gave him other jobs, and now I have to link people up with connecting transport all by my lonesome. I don't mind. I get a kick out of letting the good guys pick their rides."

She stood and gestured over her shoulder with her thumb. "Like Bud back there?" she whispered. "He's a great guy, a real gentleman, and he deserves to be taken to the river in his own beloved truck."

I looked up and over her shoulder. Sure enough, a shadowy form now occupied the passenger side of the truck. I turned to look behind me, where I'd just left Bud at the wheel of the Olds. No one was in the Olds. I'd left my door open, so there was no mistaking the long, empty expanse of yellowish vinyl bench seat. As I watched, the keys to the Olds gradually materialized until they lay sprawled on the dashboard.

When I looked back, she was staring at the Bic dangling from my fingers. I hadn't had the gumption to pocket it.

"Uh, listen, I promised Cherry Berry I'd tell you something." She looked around, chewing her thumbnail, then leaned closer to whisper, "We both signed confidentiality agreements when we got our jobs with the transportation and delivery department, but we both break the rules sometimes, our little protest now that working conditions have gone downhill. We seldom get paid, we have no backup help, et cetera. Anyway, this is confidential and CB and I would both be in trouble if our boss knew I'd . . . blabbed."

She dropped her cigarette butt and ground it out with the toe of her boot. "Okay. Nearly everybody has some little thing to say when they're crossing the river. Last thoughts, pleas to be spared, mournful songs, angry accusations. It's strictly against the confidentiality rules to divulge a pickup's last words on the trip or upon disembarking, but Cherry Berry has a lot of lapses, lots more than I have, and is always bragging about what they say or scream when they see him, the guardian of the underworld, teeth bared, three heads. Anyway, he wanted you to hear what your friend told him, the red-haired one, Trey." She leaned even closer. "As Trey got from the boat, he asked Cherry Berry to tell you that he wasn't going to let you drive that last stretch from the zinc mine fields to the bonfire. He said if Cherry Berry took you the green Bic lighter, it would prove it since you'd know he, Trey that is, only bought new cigs and brought along his lighter when he planned to make a grand entrance behind the wheel of his car, smoking. He said you were, let's see . . . something, something, and you would go nuts if CB didn't take you the lighter and give you that message."

I was frozen, rooted. My eyes burned and I had to struggle to keep my chin from quivering like a small child's. "Did he say I was an 'innocent wonder'?" I finally croaked out.

She frowned. "Nah, that wasn't it. Oh! I remember. He said you were 'awesomely loyal,' that was it. 'Tucker is awesomely loyal and he'll go nuts if he doesn't know.' I remember because Cherry Berry and I didn't think there was such a word as 'awesomely.'"

I just stood there, my chest on fire and my throat burning, so I couldn't speak.

"Well, time to travel," she said. She crawled into the driver's seat of the truck. She put her boot to the gas pedal and looked down at me.

"Last chance to come with." She snorted a laugh. "Just kidding!"

I strained to see Bud, and by letting my eyes go unfocused, I could make out the shadowy contours of his proud chin and his few flyaway head hairs.

I raised my hand to tell him good-bye, but he didn't respond. Bud was never one for sentimental leave-takings.

"You gotta officially sign off with a negative," the weird hitchhiker, that Charon, called down to me. "The standard gesture will do, just to show headquarters you're officially rescinding the pickup call."

I solemnly shook my head as Bud must have done on his long-ago battlefield. She gave me a nod and a thumbs-up to show that was acceptable, then she gave it some gas.

I watched them rattle through the wheat, cutting a narrow road as they went. When they were maybe a hundred yards away, the dog, Cerberus, materialized in the truck bed and watched me, eagerly lolling all three tongues like dogs do when they expect you to throw them a treat.

They kept going and going through the long expanse of unbroken, trackless wheat, angling slightly upward until at some point they must have reached the sky. I could see them as a shrinking black speck against the clouds for quite a while.

And then at some point, I couldn't.

I dropped to my knees then with my face tilted toward the sky and my arms stretched open. I let out a howl that went on and on. I felt pain everywhere, inside and out. It was flowing through me like I was a tiny part of a wire connecting all the grief and regret and hope and fear of the right side of the world to all those same things on the left side.

I didn't even notice the farmer who stopped his gigantic combine and came running to help me. It was nearly dark by then, and he told me at first he thought I was praying.

I didn't correct him. I have prayed off and on all my life and none of it felt anything like this. Still, maybe it was supposed to.

XIV

I WAS AT the Nebraska Medical Center in Omaha when Officer Stephens came into my room the next morning, settled into a chair beside my bed, and listened to my whole story from the time I'd found Bud unconscious in his troll-surrounded car back in the yard in Clevesdale to . . . well, the whole story. I hadn't planned on ever telling anyone about the hitchhiker girl, the flood, the black truck. But Officer Stephens deserved better than a mouthful of mumbled lies like I'd given him the night of the wreck. When I finished, he didn't say anything.

I wondered if he believed me. I sure wouldn't have.

"So, Mr. Heisterberg was with you when you located the body?" he finally asked.

I guess police get used to saying things like that, but it took me by surprise and I winced. "Yeah, he turned off his combine and we went into the house and found Bud still sitting in his chair by the broken window in that upstairs bedroom. I borrowed Mr. Heisterberg's phone and called you instead of Janet because I figured it'd be good if she heard it in person, from a friend."

He folded his arms and nodded. "I appreciate that," he said. "Good thinking."

Officer Stephens hadn't even asked me on the phone if he should drive Janet up here. He'd just told me that he'd be doing it and they'd be here in three or four hours unless Janet wanted to wait until morning, which he very much doubted she would. They'd arrived last night, while I was being treated. They'd come by the hospital, been told to come back in the morning, then driven out to the Heisterbergs'. Mrs. Heisterberg had invited them to stay overnight so Janet could more easily make funeral arrangements.

"After Mr. Heisterberg called the coroner from the old house and the body was picked up, he brought you in his truck directly here, right? To this hospital?"

I nodded. I hadn't argued when Mr. Heisterberg had strongly suggested it. It was obvious even to me by then that my legs had become infected, big-time. As they prepped me last night, they kept telling me the treatment they'd be doing would hurt a lot, but it hadn't hurt nearly as much as my legs had all on their own for the past couple of days.

Now I was bandaged from thigh to ankle up and down both legs, and I was attached to an IV of antibiotics. One strict nurse had mentioned I'd be lucky if I didn't end up needing skin grafts down the line. No one here was one bit happy with me.

It was touch-and-go whether they'd even let me out in time for the graveside funeral, which was this afternoon.

"I guess this was stupid," I mentioned, dipping my head to indicate my legs.

Officer Stephens grimaced, then gave a small smile. "Pretty much."

"Is Janet . . . here?" I asked Officer Stephens. "I mean, here at the hospital?"

He crossed his arms. "You boys had her plenty worried," he said gruffly.

I nodded and looked down at the little hoop house that framed my legs, keeping the blankets from touching my bandages. My eyes began burning and things went blurry.

He walked to the door, and when he opened it, Janet pretty much fell into the room. I guess I expected she'd have plenty to say, but she just eased herself between the bed and the IV cart, then dropped forward to sprawl across the pillows, cradling my head in her strong waitress arms with her ear settled like a suction cup against my forehead.

After a while she kissed my cheek and let me go, then pulled herself up to sit on the edge of the mattress, where for a long time she just looked solemnly down at me, pushing my hair from my face. I closed my eyes and relaxed into her stroke, like I remember doing when I'd come home banged up from stupid bike stunts in fourth grade. I felt tears burning against the backs of my eyelids.

"Oh, Tucker," she whispered sadly, "you often seem as young and breakable to me as when you were eight years old. You probably don't remember, but sometimes your dad went out by himself at night even back then. And Bud was no good as a babysitter after his bedtime at nine o'clock, so if I had to work the night shift, I used to go talk to your mother's picture. I'd just tell her I was about to leave, and I'd ask her to be there through the night for you. We've always been in cahoots, darling boy, me and Cynthia Anne. It's why I wanted her picture hung higher, so you'd see her and know that even during this awful time, your mother that you loved so dearly is still nearby, protecting you."

She sat up straight then and grabbed a bunch of hospital tissues. She buried her face in them as Officer Stephens came and took her elbow and eased her back off the high bed and around that wobbling IV cart.

I grabbed her wrist right before she got out of range. "I know my mom is nearby, Janet. I always know that's exactly where you are."

There was a lot more I wanted to tell her, like that everything in this beautiful treasure house of a world breaks, and sometimes things break so bad all you can do is hope to get your heart to stop bleeding long enough for you to sift through the ashes so you can try to gain some slight understanding. But some things that break real bad can be mended if you're lucky enough to have someone on your side with a ton of glue who won't give up.

I couldn't get any of that said, but from the look on her face, I guess I'd said enough for right then.

There were folding chairs put up under the ancient oak trees at Bud's family cemetery for the funeral. The preacher at the Heisterbergs' Methodist church read scripture, and then it was nice the way people told funny and interesting stories about Bud, how he'd been as a boy and then a young man. Janet had cousins to sit and cry with, so Officer Stephens and I just sat together a little to the side, pretty much unnecessary.

And then it was over, and Janet wanted time with her relatives, so Officer Stephens and I got into his police cruiser and drove toward Bud's old house along a nearly invisible rough road that Officer Stephens somehow located beneath the blowing wheat. Had that road been there all along, or had it been blazed just yesterday by Bud's great old black truck as it made its final journey from home, the place where Bud's own long and colorful trail had begun?

Officer Stephens parked the Olds in front of the house and we crossed the overgrown yard. He settled himself on the next-to-bottom porch step and, after a bit of hesitation, I managed to drop down onto that step as well. He propped his elbows on his knees. It felt less painful to me to keep my bandaged legs out straight, like I had at Bud's services.

"How ya' doing?" he asked with a half smile.

I gave him one back. "Those painkillers they gave me work great," I allowed.

We automatically began staring straight ahead, hypnotized by the endlessly moving grain.

It went from being afternoon to being early evening. The air lost most of its warmth, and the purple shadow of the house reached far into the wheat.

I finally heard him draw in a deep breath. "Well, we oughta get back," he said. "Janet'll be needing us. She was awful upset when I told her about Bud. He was an old guy with a bum heart, but the fact is, it's always a sad shock when it happens."

I nodded, then instead of getting up to leave as he'd suggested, we both just sat there staring across the fields to where the glint of cars marked the cemetery. He passed his police hat absently from hand to hand, as he'd been doing ever since we'd first sat down.

"Well," he said, and this time he stood, put on his hat, and began walking toward the police cruiser. Even from the back he looked trustworthy. Something in his shoulders.

"Officer Stephens?" I called. "You go on ahead. I don't think Janet should be driving right now, you know? So I'll drive the Olds back home."

He knew from my story that I'd failed my designated driver test and had lost my focus and my nerve, so I think I expected him to nix that idea. Maybe I even *hoped* he would. The hospital had only released me on the provision that I check in with the Clevesdale Clinic by tomorrow, so my physical condition for driving a car wasn't that great either.

"Right," he said, giving Bud's old car a glance. "Got those

horse-choker antibiotics the hospital gave you? And the heavy-duty Tylenol?"

I took both bottles from the pocket of the jacket Janet had brought for me to wear to the funeral. I held them up.

He nodded and got into his cruiser, then rolled down the window. "You want to follow us back?"

I shook my head. "I need to go by and thank the Heisterbergs. I'll be along after that, though. Tell Janet not to worry, I won't be more than an hour behind you."

That was the only untrue thing I told Officer Stephens that day. I'd already thanked the Heisterbergs and told them good-bye. What I needed was to be there at the old house for a little while longer, to say my own good-bye to Bud.

"Well," said Officer Stephens. And then he just kept looking at me through his open window. "Tucker, I'm not gonna ask if you'll be safe on the road going back to Oklahoma. The drive won't be easy for you, but it's never gonna get easier than it is right now. And I gotta say, the story you told me this morning at the hospital is far-fetched, still . . ." He drummed his fingers on the side of the car door and frowned.

"Thing is, Tucker, that part about the cigarette lighter? We've seen it a thousand times at the station. Some kid that doesn't smoke will buy Saturday night smokes as a pickup device, to make the girls think he's bad boy cool when he drives up. Chances are real good Trey wouldn't have let you drive down to the beach, no matter how drunk he was or if you'd stayed cold sober. He had that car to show off with, and you can't do that unless you're behind the wheel when you arrive at the party."

I just stared back at him.

"Right," he said, and started the ignition. "Don't beat yourself up so bad, that's all, Tucker. This past week was likely the worst you'll ever have in your life. Take what you can learn from it, make it a part of the code you go by, then give it the gas and get back in gear again. Janet needs you, you know."

Then he raised a hand to say good-bye and drove toward Janet, picking his way along that same rutted road he and I had traveled earlier. Actually, from the way the police car was bucking and tossing, I started wondering if that rough track should have been called a road at all. No matter who, or what, had made that passageway through the wheat, it was probably most accurate to just think of it as one of many hardscrabble byways blazed along the Oregon Trail, better known by us mortals as trail number 11,404.

I sat watching Officer Stephens's dust and wondered, what did he mean, make it a part of the code I went by? I didn't *have* a code. Did regular people have one, or just policemen?

Before the bonfire I would have defined myself as being in control of myself, of my thoughts and emotions, but that wasn't what you'd call a code, and it wasn't even accurate, at least if you knew me well, like Trey did. Neither was Trey's "innocent wonder" idea. Not a code, and not accurate, then or now. Trey surely knew that too.

I went slowly to the Olds, not bothering to put on a wellness act like I had during the funeral. I was hunched forward at the waist like I was about a hundred years old, and I moved with both legs stiff like some zombie from a laughably bad movie.

I opened the driver's-side door and was nearly overwhelmed by Bud's smell of Burma-Shave and foot powder. For the first time I noticed that where the driver sat, the sagging beige bench seat was molded to Bud's shape. I slid in beneath the steering wheel, conforming my legs, rear, and back to where Bud's had been for so many thousands of miles. Bud was far wider than me through the hips and shoulders, but that was all to the good. The lumps and ridges Bud had worn into the thin beige plastic held me in place but gave me the room I needed to stretch and shift with those thick bandages.

I reached across and thumbed the button on the glove compartment door. It flipped open and disgorged its contents, much as it had when Bud had opened it, searching for the map. I leaned on my right elbow to stir the pile of small junk now covering the passenger-side floor.

I found an old broken pencil and used my thumbnail to give it a point. I spotted an old wadded up napkin with what looked like ancient mustard staining one corner. I unfolded that napkin, spread it on the dashboard, and worked some of the wrinkles out.

Then I left that paper napkin waiting there, while I sat back and took a long breath. I looked up at the sky and focused on where I'd seen the truck disappear into the distance. I took my time, just sitting there and remembering, smiling as I did.

"I read you loud and clear, Bud," I finally whispered, and I bent toward the dashboard and began to write.

Officer Stephens was right. The drive home wasn't easy, and I knew the worst part would come last, so I dreaded it the whole way. When you're heading west into Oklahoma from Missouri, you can't help but see the ring of silver hills rising from the zinc mine fields. Gravel mountains that glow against the sky, a dreamscape, magical.

Six nights ago I'd been drinking with my friends inside the secret ring of those counterfeit mountains. *They'll always loom,* I thought as I drove right toward them, my hands so sweaty they were slipping on the wheel. *You'll always know they're out there.*

The inside of the dark car was bathed in eerie green light from the instrument panel. Everything glowed, strangely fluorescent, and blood began to beat painfully in my ears.

I took the rearview mirror and turned it toward myself, then looked into it and sat straighter until the top of my head . . .

I punched the mirror aside just in time. The next day my knuckles were bruised and they stayed bruised for a while, reminding me never to do that again.

The house was filled with people all that weekend, mostly Janet's friends and fellow waitresses, some old guys Bud had played cards with, the neighbors, including the Brandywines. A couple of police officers came with Officer Stephens on Saturday afternoon and he came alone on Sunday afternoon. The lady at the driver's license office who'd had to give Bud three separate vision tests and tell him three separate times in a row that he'd flunked came and cried and said she'd felt just awful doing that, and Janet told her she was extremely grateful to her because the last thing Bud needed was to be driving. People brought tons of food, so much it wouldn't all fit in the refrigerator.

I kept going out to the hoop house, harvesting anything that was ready. It was comforting to be able to make big salads to go with all those casseroles.

It's what happens when somebody dies. At least, I guess it is. People come over and bring food and say how sorry they are and maybe cry together.

I went to the clinic Saturday afternoon, got my bandages changed and set up an appointment for three days later. Then I tried to hang around downstairs, thinking it was the polite thing to do. But by late Sunday morning I couldn't stand it. I told Janet I was going outside and she could call me if she wanted me, I'd stay close enough to hear her.

She took my face in her hands. "You okay?" she asked.

"Yeah, yeah," I said, and I grabbed a spade and went across the street to even up the muddy ruts in Mrs. Brandywine's yard so it'd be ready for some new nasturtiums. Then I drove the Olds into our backyard and washed and polished it. Then I went inside and dug out the vacuum, brought it out to clean the vinyl floor mats. I couldn't bear to throw any of the junk on the floor away, so I stuffed it back inside the glove compartment.

Then I drove the Olds into the garage and drove Janet's Taurus into the backyard and washed and polished and vacuumed it.

Now what? I admitted to myself I'd been avoiding my room, but with the outside tasks caught up, it was either there or downstairs. Anyhow, what was I afraid of? Trey's rock was still on the windowsill, jiggling, but I'd slept up there for the past two nights with it doing that, so why did I dread going up there now, in broad daylight?

Because it was time to *do* something about Trey's rock, *that's* why.

Before I could think about it any longer, I took the stairs quickly, and once inside my room I jerked my desk chair over against the window, then immediately straddled it backward and stared down at the pebble with my forehead against the glass.

"So, Trey? What're you trying to tell me, buddy? Are you saying you wouldn't have let me drive, there at the end? Because you wanted to make an entrance? Did you really call me loyal, buddy? If I knew that was true, it would mean the world to me. But I could sure understand it if you're angry instead. But, well . . . either way, we both have to move on, and I can't do it until you do it."

"Tucker?"

I jumped up, toppling the chair, and whirled around to see Mrs. Beetlebaum standing in my doorway. For a few seconds I couldn't remember how to think and I just stood there gawking at her, not truly comprehending who she was. For one thing, she wasn't wearing one of her long dark dresses or her black leather school shoes. She had on a pair of brown slacks and a light purple sweater and white socks with small cats embroidered on them and Birkenstock sandals, I think is what you call them.

"Oh, I'm so sorry to have startled you, Tucker!" She put up her hands, then she smiled and clasped them behind her and took a step forward. "I *did* knock, and your mother said it would be fine to come on up and pay my respects."

"No! I mean, *yes*, thanks, come in!" I grabbed the chair and stood it on its feet.

Mrs. Beetlebaum began walking slowly around my room, her long hair trickling down her back like a silver waterfall. She looked at all my stuff with a bright smile. Even when she stopped to take in the shelf where I keep my collection of worn-out running shoes, she looked like someone studying a painting at some fancy art gallery.

"I keep . . . thinking I may need those," I explained weakly. The best of those pairs looked like something that had been run over a few times by a bulldozer or something.

"Things contain memories," she said. "They become more than mere objects."

I nodded, glad she understood. I'd won a race in each of those pairs.

Mrs. Beetlebaum moved on to the bulletin board I'd had since third grade. I used to have it covered with stuff, but I

214

hadn't used it in a while. Yesterday, though, I'd tacked the list I made at Bud's old house up there.

"Uh, Mrs. Beetlebaum?" I said to her back as she read the list. "I . . . don't need your coin any longer. I was going to give it back to you at school tomorrow. I've kind of, like, got some questions about it?" Only about a million.

"I'll bet you have," she murmured, but she didn't turn, just kept reading. The list wasn't long, but the pencil had been pretty shoddy, so it was taking her a while. I walked to my backpack and yanked out the jeans I'd worn to Nebraska. They were stiff and rank, a total mess. I felt for Trey's lighter and found it easily, but the obolus was stuck by a glob of mud to the pocket it was in.

I finally worked it loose and put the lighter and the muddy coin together on my math book, which was lying with some other stuff on the side of my bed I don't use.

Mrs. Beetlebaum finished reading and totally surprised me by coming over and actually sitting on my messy bed, right beside the math book. She looked down at the obolus, then picked it up, holding it between her thumb and forefinger.

"You met the ferryman, then," she said with a mysterious smile. "I'm not *sure* how the whole thing works, Tucker, but I can tell you what I *think* happens."

I yanked my desk chair over close to where she sat, then dropped into it like a little kid grabbing the last seat on the bus. I had never in my life been so ready to listen.

XV

BUT BEFORE SHE BEGAN her promised explanation, she leaned close and squinted at me, looking me over carefully, especially my face. "Yes, yes, you look . . . clearer. Sad, of course. Yes, sad, maybe I'd go on to say heartbroken, but much, much clearer."

I'd noticed that myself in the bathroom mirror. I was pale and sort of bruised-looking under my eyes, but the thing that had been living *inside* my eyes had moved out.

"My father-in-law, Karl, gave this coin to me, Tucker. In fact, he urgently *pressed* it upon me much as I pressed it upon you. He was an archaeologist and worked for much of his career on a group of islands in the Aegean Sea. One fateful day, when he'd been working in Greece for several months without bothering to visit home, he received a letter from the States sent by his wife, my husband's mother, telling him she was divorcing him and marrying another man. Karl said he realized too late that he'd ignored his family for the sake of his career, and he felt such bitter regret he could barely walk, or think, or remember to feed himself or sleep.

"Karl had a co-worker who became very worried about him, especially when he began making dangerous mistakes on the job, even causing small landslides at their work site two different times. This man, this worried co-worker, was Greek, and one day he came to Karl and pushed this coin into his hand." She shrugged. "Karl was told that he must keep the coin in his pocket and not surrender it under any circumstances, just as I told *you* when I gave you the obolus."

Mrs. Beetlebaum put the coin back onto its little nest of mud there on my math book. She folded her arms. "Picture a beautiful energy inside you. See it as a flowing golden ribbon, the unbroken ribbon of life that keeps one moving, making plans, laughing at jokes and smelling flowers, even feeling the sort of authentic, human sadness that eventually turns to memory and heals the heart. Now picture that precious ribbon snapped in two, broken quickly and cleanly, like anything else wound too tightly. Only drastic measures may realign the two ends to reconnect that flow.

"That's where the obolus comes in. There aren't that many of these around now, though in classical times they were common, placed in the mouths of practically everyone who died. The ferryman never got over wanting that payment, so these attract him, and once he comes for you, you're forced to, well, snap out of it. That is, you're forced to make the decision to reconnect with life. It's like a cosmic slap in the face. Yes, I think that's the best I can explain it. You must reconnect with life or . . ."

She left it at that, so I finished her sentence. "Or surrender the obolus and . . . die?"

She sighed. "Yes, I think that's about the size of it. Strong medicine, yes? But as I said, drastic situations require drastic measures. I doubt a person can live long anyway with that vital energy flow broken. One becomes almost, well, a sleepwalker, unable to respond to life's many demands and challenges. Karl, for instance, might easily have gotten co-workers killed with his inattention to the dangerous ground he and the other archaeologists on his team were excavating at the time."

I frowned, confused. "But how do you think that ribbon thing gets wound too tight in the first place?"

She took hold of my wrist and leaned very close. "I think by a shock releasing too many powerful emotions—guilt, grief, regret? Karl gave the coin to *me* two weeks after my husband, his son, died of cancer. I would not say I was exactly suicidal, but I dreamed every night about going across the darkness to Theo, taking his hand and bringing him back up to the world of light with me. Or else in my dreams I'd stay with him there, wherever he was. I wished my days away, waiting only for night to come, when I could again live in my dreams. So yes, the ribbon of life inside me had snapped, though I was only aware of being in a sort of chilly daze. Someone who's been there must recognize the symptoms *for* you, you see. You're too numb to know anything yourself. *You* certainly were too numb, weren't you, Tucker?"

Mrs. Beetlebaum patted my hand and slid from my bed. She went to stand at my window with her back to me.

"The day after Karl slipped the obolus into my jacket pocket, I was in the public library, where I worked at that time," she said. "I was listlessly pushing the book cart from aisle to aisle, shelving books, when I turned into the Mythology section and, well, there it was. The ferryman."

She turned to me. "How did it appear to you, Tucker? As male? Female?"

"Female. A girl with knobby knees and a motorcycle jacket. Pink hair and attitude. Red cowboy boots."

She smiled and nodded. "I perceived it as a platinum blond woman of about thirty years, dressed in an inappropriately filmy and low-cut silver evening dress, bloodred lipstick, heavy false eyelashes, and what appeared to be real diamond jewelry, a bracelet and earring set. Marilyn Monroe was all the rage then, and this entity turned to me and said, in a breathy voice *exactly* like Marilyn's, 'In six minutes, using your human measurements, the window beneath the big clock in the library reading room will be hit by a rock thrown up by a lawn mower. It'll shatter just all *over* the place.' And then, as if this weren't strange enough, she winked one of those heavy-lashed eyes at me and asked, 'Do you think I'm as glamorous as a movie star? Or do you think I'd be even *more* glamorous with different eyes, maybe diamond ones?'"

I jabbed the air with my finger. "Yes, absolutely, Mrs. Beetlebaum! That was *her!*"

Mrs. Beetlebaum laughed. "You know, it's interesting that she wore red cowboy boots when she appeared to you, because she wore red high heels when she appeared to me. And Karl, before he died, told me she appeared to him in a ruffled black and purple dress that was short enough to expose red velvet lace-up boots of the sort generally worn by women of his generation, though in black, certainly not in scarlet. He said she looked like a dance hall girl. It embarrassed poor Karl to even say 'dance hall girl' to me."

I shook my head, still boggled by all this. "So what'd you do when you came face-to-face with her?"

Mrs. Beetlebaum turned back to the window. "Well, at first I assumed she was just some kook," she said. "A library must expect and welcome even the most eccentric people, so I simply pushed my book cart back out the way I'd come, thinking I'd wait until she'd gone away before I shelved the books in that aisle. Oddly enough, though, something *did* make me go into the reading room, where I asked the two young men seated there to move into a different location. When the window in that room was hit by a rather large rock about three minutes later, all the ivy plants kept on that windowsill were shattered, as was the goldfish bowl on the desk beneath it. We barely managed to retrieve the three little goldfish in time. Once we settled them into a new container of water, the white one appeared not to feel well. So of course I took him between my thumb and forefinger and gently pinched his little sides pepeatedly as I sailed him slowly through the water, giving him artificial respiration. He rallied, I'm happy to say."

Mrs. Beetlebaum suddenly bent forward and crossed her arms. "Tucker, it's the strangest thing, there's a pebble on your window ledge that's been . . . moving, dancing around. Would you come over here and take a look?"

I skulked over and glanced down at the pebble, trying to seem casual. "Well, see, that's Trey's rock. He had a can of those in his car, and he used to throw a handful up at my window when he wanted me." Then suddenly, panic and sorrow ambushed me and I blurted, "I don't know what I can do for him, Mrs. Beetlebaum, and he can't *tell* me! I want to just . . . well, to just flick the rock away so it won't haunt me like it's doing, but I can't do that either because it would be like flicking Trey away! So I just have to leave it out there and Trey keeps . . . keeps jiggling and jiggling it like that!"

Mrs. Beetlebaum stood straight and looked up to meet my eyes. I thought I'd see ridicule or disbelief in her expression, but she just seemed puzzled by how upset I was.

"But isn't it obvious? Here. Open the window."

I hung back, biting my lip like a scared little preschooler.

"Tucker, please, just open it."

So I did, I jerked the window up, bracing myself for the rock to, what? Attack me?

Mrs. Beetlebaum reached down, picked up the rock, then lifted one of my hands. "Trey just wants you to treat this memento of your friendship like one of those prized racing shoes of yours." She put the pebble on my palm. "Keep it somewhere special and think of him when you see it. *That's* all he wants from you."

I stood there staring down at my hand as a tidal wave of relief and new grief surged through my tangled brain and began making its way into my bloodstream. After a couple of minutes, I very carefully closed my fingers around Trey's last rock.

I didn't even notice that Mrs. Beetlebaum had left my side until she asked from across the room, "Tucker, what *is* this extraordinary document you have posted?"

I jerked up my head to see her reading Bud's list again. "It's some stuff Bud told me about driving and cars." I cleared my throat and asked, "Mrs. Beetlebaum, do you think that list might be called, well, a code Bud went by when he drove?"

She took off her glasses and dropped them to dangle on this chain she had around her neck. "I once lost twelve dollars to Bud, playing poker at the senior center downtown. He was such fun, and it's a shame his heart kept him cooped up at home in his final years. Yes, this sounds like his rules of the road, the code he drove by, and lived by."

So she'd known Bud? I don't know why that surprised me, but it sort of did.

She walked to my desk chair and sat down, then sighed and straightened her shoulders. "Well, Tucker, let me quickly finish telling you about Marilyn Monroe. I find myself tiring easily lately."

I went to sit on the bed, close to the chair so she wouldn't have to talk very loud. Also, I could hand her the obolus in case she forgot to take it with her.

"Well, let's see," she began. "It was closing time that same day at the library, about five o'clock. The head librarian sent me to look for tardy patrons in the restrooms, down all the aisles, in the basement children's section, the usual places. I remember I came upon someone trying to finish reading an article on tennis in the periodicals room and urged him along, but otherwise the place was empty except for the three of us workers and the library cat, Dickens. My co-workers both had places to be, families to take care of, but I did not. I was utterly solitary and could only look forward to a dinner of fish sticks and asparagus, then an evening of watching public television as I yearned for bedtime and my dreams of Theo. So I told my boss I would stay for a few minutes and lock up after the tennis reader had finished. Presently, he did just that, finished the article and left through the turnstile. I locked the front door behind him, as I had already locked the back entrance to prevent late patrons from slipping in unnoticed.

"I decided to give the poor traumatized goldfish a final pinch of food, then I took my own coat and scarf from the little closet behind the circulation desk. I walked the length of the library as I wound my scarf, checking things once more, then I went through the lobby toward the front door, which was actually a double door, made entirely of glass. I mention this because I suddenly saw the reflection of the ferryman in that glass. It was following close behind me, gliding across the floor as though on wheels. It was huge, perhaps nine feet tall, all greenish in color, a shadowy presence concealed within a moldy cloak. I felt its cold breath as an icy wind along my neck, felt it right through my heavy scarf. My skin crawled and my heart raced, and though I was tempted to run that last several feet to the door, I knew I could not hope to escape my . . . pursuer.

"So I stopped and turned to face it, and in that split second it was able to slip into its glamorous facade again. The red heels, the filmy dress, the wild and loose platinum hair, the eyelashes—everything was the same except for the eyes. Its two eye sockets were now fitted with huge multi-faceted diamonds. No pupils, no irises, just two dazzling rocks. It came very close to me and said, in a breathy little-girl voice, 'Diamonds are a girl's best friend, know what I mean?' And then it fastened those diamond eyes on me and *mesmerized* me, I guess you'd say. I don't know how long I stood there mere inches from it, locked in place while it probed my deepest, most aching memories of . . . Theo."

Mrs. Beetlebaum suddenly slumped forward and covered her face with her hands.

I was pretty sure she was just upset, not really sick or anything like that, but I had no clue what to do for her. "Uh, Mrs. Beetlebaum, are you okay? I could go get you a drink of water, or how about a snack? Somebody brought some of those sliders, like little tiny hamburgers with picante sauce all over them?"

Too late, I remembered eating the last three or four of those.

But she didn't want them anyhow. She shook her head fast, almost like she was shivering.

"No, thank you, Tucker," she whispered as she took a tissue from her sweater pocket. She dabbed at her eyes, then blew her nose. "I'll be just fine in a moment."

I nodded and waited. "The crazy hitchhiker girl did that to me too," I told her quietly. "I mean the ferryman, that Charon? She, it, I mean? It somehow locked into my thoughts through my eyes so I'd tell it my . . . memories of the wreck and stuff."

Mrs. Beetlebaum blew her nose again, then smiled at me in a sad way.

"Well, Tucker, I suppose that's just . . . what happens, yes? The ferryman reads your life after a combination of sadness and the obolus draws him to confront you. And what he sees there helps him figure how to get you to surrender the coin. I don't know how long I stood there, reliving the best days of my life, when Theo and I were so happy, and also reliving the worst, the dark days since Theo's death. But I remember while I was still locked into that strange state, I began to hear the ocean, first faintly and then more and more insistently. It was the sound of my most wonderful memory, the sound of our honeymoon, mine and Theo's, there on the Gulf of Mexico, in Florida. We had a tiny cabana for two weeks, right on the beach. A little green rowboat came with the package. And always, day and night, there was the mysterious, delicious sound of those waves."

She squinted and shook her head. "But it was so very strange.

I'd been *remembering* that sound, but then suddenly I heard the hum of the fluorescent lights as well and I knew I was awakening from my trance and coming back to the library. I smelled the books and looked down to see the scuffed tile floor, but when I looked straight ahead of me, all was lost in swirling, murky shadows. And *still* there was the sound of those waves breaking upon the beach somewhere quite, quite close.

"Then the Marilyn Monroe entity materialized a few feet in front of me, her eyes simply blue eyes again. She held out her hand and said to me, in that breathy voice, 'Give me what you have in your pocket and I'll take you where you long to go.' And then she took several steps backward with her hand still out, like a TV hostess revealing some prize behind a curtain. And the swirling shadows parted so that I was suddenly staring right at the Gulf of Mexico, there where the library computer bank usually was. There where the big pink dinosaur sign ordinarily stood, directing patrons to the children's room downstairs. It was now all churning water, and there was the evocative sound of seagulls, and there was a little green boat drifting in the distance, and . . . and . . ."

She closed her eyes and said in an urgent whisper, "My hand found my pocket and I clasped the obolus as hard as I could! Oh, how I *yearned* to pay the fare so I might sail away to the land I dreamed of, where my lost love was waiting for me!"

Mrs. Beetlebaum slowly turned her head to look down at the obolus there on my bed. She sat very still, her eyes glistening with longing as she clasped her hands in her lap and held them so tightly they shook. I knew she was standing on that dark shore in the landlocked library again. She longed to take back the coin, to make the decision she hadn't made that day when she'd had the clear opportunity.

I knew all that because I was feeling that longing again myself. I had to shove my hands hard into my pockets to keep from reaching for that coin. I wondered if I could ever give up the feeling that I should have been with them, should have been the fourth guy to make the set complete, and also in some strange way to look after them. Could I give up that feeling when it would mean I was giving up the best friends I would ever have, saying good-bye in some more complete way than I could imagine doing? Could I ever figure out how to do that, to say good-bye and still remember? Could she give up the sad dreams she dreamed of recovering her lost love? Doubtful in both cases.

This wasn't good. I gathered a breath, then whispered, "Uh, Mrs. Beetlebaum?"

She jerked, startled, then gave a deep sigh and used the chair arms to raise herself to a slow stand. "I must get to a yoga class tonight," she murmured, clucking her tongue as she slowly straightened her back. "I missed two evenings last week and it has me stiff."

She touched the knuckles of my hand, the one with Trey's rock. "Keep that safe," she said, then she gave me a wink and walked to the door. "I'll see you tomorrow at school, Tucker."

"Wait, Mrs. Beetlebaum! You didn't say why you *didn't* give up the coin!"

She had her hand on the doorknob, but she turned. "Actually, Tucker, it was the library cat, Dickens. As I stood entranced by the roiling water and that dear green boat, I felt Dickens winding himself around my ankles, and when I glanced down at him, he looked up at me with the expression cats have when they need you for something. He had just eaten, so I knew he simply wanted to be petted, and without thinking about it, I crouched and ran my hands over his sleek gray fur. And, well, I found I didn't want to put my hand back into my pocket then. The coin was just too cold after the particular warmth that only comes from warm, beating, purring life."

I picked up the obolus and wiped most of the mud on the hem of my T-shirt. "You almost forgot this, Mrs. Beetlebaum." I hurried to her, holding it out.

But when I reached her, she put her hands on my shoulders and whispered, "Shall I tell you what *truly* happened, Tucker?" She narrowed her eyes, giving me a sly smile. "Dickens wound himself around my ankles, and I crouched to stroke him. He began to purr, and I suddenly had the most vivid memory of a small event from the early days of my marriage. I was still a college student when we married, struggling to pay my tuition from my library salary. Theo and I were in the park one summer afternoon, eating ice cream cones. There was a skinny little yellow stray kitten following us, and I found a large leaf and broke him off a chunk of my ice cream and cone. And while we crouched there watching the kitten eat, I mentioned to Theo that I was thinking I might quit school so I could use my salary at the library to help with our apartment rent. And Theo adamantly shook his head and leaned close to push my hair behind my ear. 'You can't quit school, you're a born teacher,' he said. 'You'll see. Teaching will be the love of your life.' He himself was a math teacher, which made him a bit of an authority. I rolled my eyes and even laughed, I think, but because of what he'd said, I didn't quit school. I was in my last semester when he died."

Mrs. Beetlebaum gave my shoulders a squeeze, then released me. "Teaching *has* been the love of my life, Tucker, second only to Theo. I believe Theo somehow communicated that small but life-changing ice cream moment to me, through Dickens. And that's what made me keep the obolus in my pocket and long for life again."

She turned back to the door, opened it, and stepped through. "I am so sorry for your loss, Tucker. Bud was a fine man." She waved good-bye over her shoulder.

"Mrs. Beetlebaum, you forgot the obolus!"

"It stays with *you* now, Tucker," she said without turning. "Someday you will spot the person who should have it next. That's part of the deal, so keep your eyes open, but at the same time, don't act too quickly with so much at stake!"

XVI

I STATIONED MYSELF at the kitchen sink that night and washed the dishes that had been accumulating all weekend. I gave the dishwasher a complete pass and just washed everything by hand, silverware, glasses, everything. I took my time. The voices of the people still stopping by the house flowed over me in a soothing, monotonous way without my having to actually follow conversations like I would have had to if I'd hung around in the living room.

I used the time to try and figure out where I should keep the obolus. My pocket was no good, not even for a minute. Even there on my bed it had brought unhealthy longings to both me and Mrs. Beetlebaum. Out in the open anywhere in my room felt unsafe for that same reason and also because it might get lost, or even be thrown away by Janet on a cleaning rampage. My dresser drawers would also be subject to Janet when she put away clean clothes. The obolus looked like some video game token, some arcade souvenir. She could easily mistake it for worthless junk and decide to get rid of it.

At first, each time the dish drainer got full, I stopped washing and dried stuff myself, but at some point Officer Stephens wandered in, pulled the dish towel from my shoulder, and took over that part. I remember he mumbled a couple of times something about Janet being exhausted and he sure wished these good people would go home to bed now. I nodded and smiled from one side of my mouth, totally agreeing, but what could you do?

"Here, these are yours," he said when we'd been working silently for a while. "I almost forgot why I came in here. Janet wanted me to pass them along to you."

I glanced over. He was holding out a couple of car keys.

"Keys to the Taurus?" I nodded and kept on swabbing a coffee cup. "Thanks."

Janet had been talking about making me a set, for when she needed me to run some errand or for those occasions when I took her car to fill it or wash it. In fact, that afternoon I'd had to ask for her keys to take the Taurus around back so I could clean it.

"No, to the Olds," Officer Stephens said. He put the two keys on the drain board and picked up one of the three wet bowls waiting for his attention. "Janet says it's yours now. These keys are extras Bud had up in that old Vaseline jar where he kept his state quarter collection and his favorite chewed-up toothpick." He chuckled.

I remember I froze in place with my dishcloth wadded into that cup. The suds in the sink sparkled in a strange way, all blue and filmy. I had never in my life felt the sort of weak-kneed desire for anything I was suddenly feeling for Bud's car. The junk crammed into the glove compartment, the formfitting sags in the driver's seat, the green dashboard lighting, the smells of grease and sweat and hair oil, the way the wind traveled so freely through it. It was like stepping back into a time when baseball was played on dirt fields and you got root beer in a glass mug, at least if Bud's stories were to be believed.

I finally swallowed and said, "Janet needs to sell the Olds. She doesn't know how much a vintage car like that can bring these days. Everything's retro, and that car's in great condition now that the grime is off it. I mean, sure it's a gas guzzler, but it's also a classic. Somebody will buy it to drive once a week, and not far, to shows and stuff. She needs the money it'll bring. She needs to sell it."

I hadn't heard Janet come into the kitchen, but she said quietly from not far behind me, "Sweetheart, I could never sell Dad's car. He would be so proud to see you have it."

Bud, proud of me having his car? I didn't turn around. I couldn't. "You don't know everything that happened," I pushed out. "He . . . had a heart attack. I took him to the emergency room, but I couldn't make him go in. I *didn't* make him go in. All he wanted was to look for his truck, so that ended up being what we did. The *last* thing he did."

Silence. Then, Janet said, "Do you know how many times that happened to *me* with him, Tucker? At least three times I got him to the hospital parking lot and that was as far as I could get him. Other times he checked himself out of the hospital against doctor's orders. That was Dad. As he liked to say, his wounds were his own. You gave him the ride of his life, taking him up to his old farm like that. You know that, don't you?"

I braced my palms against the stainless steel rim of the sink as tears I hadn't known I had began hitting the suds, popping and scattering them, exploding them like shells falling from the sky can explode a muddy trench, can blow things into bits too small to recover. Like a great red bird of a flying car can explode into ashes that rain back down, scalding both chilly sand and fragile flesh, melting everything together so you don't know what is what. You just don't know what is . . . what.

My shoulders were heaving, but I tried not to make any noise, tried to stifle at least the sound. My mouth was open and my nose was running. I could taste salt.

I hoped no one would touch me, and they didn't.

"Janet?" I whispered. "Trey and I loved those stories of Bud's so much. I don't know why we quit listening, I guess we just grew up. But Trey remembered things from those stories all the time, like just a couple of weeks ago he reminded me of what Bud said about his dad's two mules and how they were yoked together to load walnut logs onto a railroad car. On the way to Nebraska, Bud told me more stories, and I know he knew that was exactly what I needed, his stories. I mean, Janet, I'll always be so grateful for Bud's stories, and for getting to watch his old game tapes with him. I loved that too."

I heard Janet draw in a breath and begin sobbing again, then after a few minutes I think they knew I needed to be alone, because I heard the two of them quietly leave the kitchen. They closed the door behind them, and I just kept standing there, dropping tears, destroying the suds so that I had to keep adding more detergent.

When all the visitors had finally gone home, I went out to the driveway and pulled everything out of Bud's glove compartment. I put the obolus inside, then crammed everything else back in on top of it.

So all that happened right before Halloween, and now it's almost Thanksgiving. The chamber of commerce has all the streets downtown looped with green and gold lights, and there are banners of smiling fat turkeys with Pilgrim hats giving folks a wing wave. Clevesdale spends a fortune on bizarre holiday decorations. You should see Christmas.

At school, people have made shrines of Steve, Zero, and Trey's lockers, piling stuff in front of them, starting with leftover homecoming carnations in the school colors and Halloween candy, which was finally removed when the night custodians caught a bunch of the school mice having a midnight feast. The wilted carnations are still there. There's also a lot of stuff taped to the doors, which started with these cheesy poems one of the English classes wrote. I guess I shouldn't be like that about people's poetry, but if you write about a thing like death, your words should, well, bring some uniqueness to the subject. These poems are mostly about crying, and I have a feeling that's because so much rhymes with that word, including the obvious first choice, *dying. Buying, lying, trying, denying, drying* (as in the tears you were crying), even *why-ing.* Would you believe it, four of those poems used *why-ing?* "I can't understand and so I keep why-ing." Well, who *can* understand death? Not understanding death is universal, is a given, no use going on and on about it, as Bud might have said.

One night I was doing homework at my desk when Janet knocked and came in with a clean pair of my jeans over her arm. She noticed the mustard-stained napkin on my bulletin board for the first time. "What's this?" she said, and stood there reading.

I got up and took the jeans from her, then stood beside her. "Bud's rules of the road."

She bit her bottom lip and ran her fingers under her eyes, then she started at the top and quietly read the list out loud.

"One. Never leave a lady stranded on the highway. Two. Things loom up fast, remember. Three. Keep a map in your vehicle, but know when to toss it. Four. Carry tools in the trunk and don't be tempted to take them out and use them for whatnot around the house. Five. Change the oil every three thousand miles. Six. A day of freedom on the open road beats a year cooped up inside four walls."

She turned to me and smiled. "That sounds just like him."

I've had the six things on Bud's list memorized for quite some time, but still the list stays up there. There's a narrow ledge along the bottom of the bulletin board where I keep Trey's green lighter and the last rock he threw. The rock no longer jiggles, never dances around on a windless night. He's gone from it, completely. From it, not me. I wish I could show Trey Bud's old car.

Officer Stephens picks Janet up and drives her to work now, so the Taurus stays in the garage most of the time and the Olds stays in the driveway. I keep it polished up. It's that sort of car, needs to have a shine. I like how I can see it from my window. I like how the moving leaves on the big sycamore tree in our yard are mirrored in its chrome hubcaps and along the wide bumper.

Last week I was standing at Trey's locker, reading some of those bad poems, when I felt someone nearby and glanced over to see Grace Reiser. She wrinkled her nose and said, "I think they should throw away these ugly dead carnations, don't you?" She crouched down and gathered up a handful. Her dark hair moved like water, came sliding across her shoulder. "I'm tossing some of these," she looked up and told me.

I nodded. "I don't know about some of these poems, either," I surprised myself by confiding. "But, well, I guess I don't know all that much about poetry." I shrugged.

She smiled. "Are you okay, Tucker? Can I help in any way?"

"I'm fine," I told her, then I decided on more honesty. "Well, I'm getting there."

She shifted her books, shook back her bangs, and smiled again. Then she walked on.

I was watching her go down the hall when someone clutched my elbow from behind and jerked me backward, hard. "What is *wrong* with you, Tucker?"

I turned to look into the legendary green eyes of the beautiful Aimee.

"What?" I asked. Had she forgotten what a loser she'd decided I was, that I was far too hopeless to communicate with? No, wait—she was probably here to remind me, in case I'd let the fact of my loserness momentarily slip my loser brain.

"What's up, Aimee? I gotta get to track."

She smacked her gum in a you-are-too-stupid-to-live sort of way while she explored a strand of her own hair. "Ick, a split end," she murmured, then she flipped her hair over her shoulder, folded her arms, and ran her eyes over me from head to toe, shaking her head in obvious disgust.

I had a sudden inspiration. I read somewhere that if you want an honest evaluation of yourself, you should ask an enemy. "Aimee, what do you think Trey and Steve and Zero . . . liked about me, as a friend?" This was really lame, but I was in too far to go back. "I mean, I sometimes wonder why they wanted me to hang out with them. They were so flashy and I'm . . . obviously not."

She frowned at me, then shrugged. "There's this thing that's honorable about you, like you'd try not to let anyone down. It's kind of old-fashioned, and it's really cute."

I waited for the shot of sarcasm, but she stood there like what she'd said was a given.

Then she delivered a zinger. "Tucker, you *are* a good-looking guy, especially now that your long eyelashes have grown back. Still, if it weren't for sweet Zero, I would give up on you completely, you are *that* dense. News flash! That cute girl has been hitting on you for weeks."

Something in me turned over. "Grace Reiser? No way." I snorted.

"Whatever you say, Tucker." She sashayed down the hall still shaking her head, then turned around to call to me, "I'm so sure *you're* better at reading such things than *I* am, you're such a social guru and *so* in the loop."

She had a point. And as I thought about it, I did remember a couple of things. Grace had asked me to hold her place in line once in the cafeteria, then offered to save me a seat since I would be coming through after her. And she'd called one night to get clarification on a homework assignment. Several of her girlfriends were in that class, so she could have called one of them instead. Wow. Grace Reiser.

On the other hand, Aimee might be pulling something, trying to trap me into making a fool of myself for retribution since she was convinced I'd deliberately tried to make a fool of her and her friends at the funeral. Funerals. I mean, she might have just noticed me watching Grace walk away and seen her chance to make me look stupid. Stupider.

Thing is, hanging out with Zero, Steve, and Trey so much had made me rusty where approaching girls was concerned. The girls I'd dated had basically been girls I'd gotten to know at parties or Trey's band gigs where I'd gone with the three of them. I'd just end up with a girl from some cluster of girls we all met and we'd go out for a while.

There'd been no one like Grace, though. I decided to call her, about homework.

Her mother answered. "Um, I think she's with Josh. Should I have her call you when they get back?"

"No, thanks. It's not important." I hung up the phone, glad that at least I hadn't given my name. Which Josh? Probably Josh Hinstrom. I felt gutted, hollowed out.

It turned out Grace figured out it was me who'd called from caller ID, and after school the next day she tapped me on the shoulder while I was feeding the soda machine in the gym. She was buckling on a bike helmet, which for some reason made me notice the delicate line of freckles across the bridge of her nose.

"So what'd you want when you called last night?" She smiled up at me. Her smile is great, the delivery especially. She just beams it right into you. "I was over at my cousin's and I could have called you back from there." Again, the smile.

"Your cousin . . . Josh?"

She nodded. "We were trying to make a centerpiece for the big family Thanksgiving bash, out of feathers and pinecones? It turned out really gruesome." She laughed.

"I wanted the homework assignment. No big deal. Just, you know. Math."

"Oh," she said. "Well, that's good. That it wasn't a big deal, I mean."

I nodded and grinned, but I couldn't think of anything to say, nothing at all. I was just too afraid to take a chance on doing it wrong, saying the wrong thing.

I realized right then that this was much worse than just being rusty. My confidence was gone, not that I'd ever been the most confident of people. Still, I'd had confidence that the ground would hold me up, that the sky would stay above my head.

Now, suddenly, I wasn't so sure. Would the ground hold? Could you trust the sky?

Grace bent to fold her jeans at her ankle then fastened the fold tight with her bike clip to keep the denim out of the gears, and as I watched, I made a final desperate struggle to find something, anything, to say or do. Nothing. The place where I used to keep that stuff was vacant, emptied out. No courage anywhere, no talk to talk.

She stood up, took a breath, and gave a little bounce on her heels. "Okay, that's it, then." She adjusted her helmet, then jogged through the gym and out the back door.

I watched her take her bike from the rack out there. She pedaled away, fast. She's that kind of cyclist, a competitor, a long-distance rider. *That's it, then.* The way she'd said it made me feel sick to my stomach. I chugged the orange drink I had in my hand, then crushed the can and shot it viciously into the trash can as I strode out of the school.

I sat in the car, clutching the wheel, flexing my fingers. Put it behind you. Put her behind you. Think of something immediate to do, anything. Get busy.

I usually work the Christmas season at Greenfield's, wiring together wreathes and pruning Christmas trees. So I'd fill out my application like I'd been meaning to do. That's what I'd do. I'd do it now, right now.

I didn't realize I was on Maple Street until I got to the wild soccer kids' block and had to slow to a total crawl to keep from running over a few of them. They bobbed and jumped around the car like little maniacs, but I'm not sure any of them recognized me or the Olds. Life is a series of strange events when you're that age, if I remember right. Always you're in the present, never in the past. Who could remember from clear last month a green car in Jeremy's yard with a guy maybe dead inside it? How I envied them.

Maple is the main road that goes clear through Clevesdale, but nothing takes me down it on a regular basis except when I'm working at Greenfield's. I probably should have checked before then on the three fake deer Bud had knocked over that day, but to be honest, I hadn't thought of it. Now, though, I watched for the yellow-shingled house, anxious to see if all three of those deer had survived the hit they took.

There was the house. I spotted it a block away. And there were the deer, standing where they'd stood before Bud creamed them. I slowed to a crawl again as I got nearer, checking out their details, looking to see if anything on them was broken or missing or . . .

Grace! Her bike was lying on the sidewalk, and she was bent over it on her knees, her helmet on the ground beside her. I pulled to the curb and jumped from the car.

"Grace!" I called, my heart racing. "What happened?"

"Hey, Tucker!" She stood up and took a step toward me, smiling a sheepish version of her smile. "I've got a flat. It's weird, I think I hit a plastic antler, it looks like. From those deer up there in the yard, I guess. Sliced my tire."

It's hard to describe what happened next. Something clicked inside me. I don't mean clicked in the sense of someone finally figuring out how to do algebra or even remembering how to talk to a girl. I mean clicked in the sense of I *heard* a small but distinct click, and then I felt something thick and golden speeding through my veins.

"No problem!" I called, smiling my own smile right back at her. "I've got a patch kit and an air compressor right here in my trunk."

AUTHOR'S NOTE

The idea for *Everything Breaks* came partly from a horrific drunk-driving accident that actually took place at my own high school when I was a junior. There was a closed-casket funeral for one of the boys involved, but this boy's mother understandably didn't like the way we kids were getting into the drama of the thing, thinking of it more like a movie than real life, with us as the stars. She went forward and opened her son's casket and we all got a good look at the reality of death as we filed by him on our way from the church. Believe me, that's not a thing you ever forget, and I used my memories of it as the model for the opening section of this book.

The fourth boy, Tucker, I invented, and of course I imagined up the characters from Greek mythology that are attracted to him by his instability. My parents both died in 2010, and I was grieving as I wrote this book, feeling, in many ways, much as Tucker feels. Writing is always a journey toward understanding, and this time out I wanted to know: When those you love die, what of them lasts? I found my answer, so now I can put them in place in my heart and be simply grateful for their unbreakable gifts to me.